S0-BXK-207

PENGUIN BOOKS

GEORGIA DISAPPEARED

Ellen Godfrey was born in Chicago, Illinois and
now lives in Victoria, British Columbia. Since grad-
uating from Stanford University with a BA in history and anthropology, Godfrey has made her home
in many parts of the world including Ghana,
France and several places in Ontario. She co-
founded the literary publishing house Press
Porcépic and is currently the proprietor of a computer software company. Godfrey's first three murder mysteries, *The Case of the Cold Murderer*, *Murder
Among the Well-to-do*, and *Murder Behind Locked Doors*,
have won critical acclaim, and her non-fiction
account of the 1980 murder of Betty Belshaw, *By
Reason of Doubt*, won a Special Edgar Award.

ELLEN GODFREY

A JANE TREGAR MYSTERY

GEORGIA DISAPPEARED

Penguin Books

PENGUIN BOOKS
Published by the Penguin Group
Penguin Books Canada Ltd, 10 Alcorn Avenue, Toronto, Ontario M4V 3B2
Penguin Books Ltd, 27 Wrights Lane, London W8 5TZ, England
Penguin Books USA Inc., 375 Hudson Street, New York, New York 10014,
U.S.A.
Penguin Books Australia Ltd, Ringwood, Victoria, Australia
Penguin Books (NZ) Ltd, 182-190 Wairau Road, Auckland 10, New Zealand
Penguin Books Ltd, Registered Offices: Harmondsworth, Middlesex,
England

Published in Penguin Books, 1992
Published in this edition, 1993

10 9 8 7 6 5 4 3 2 1

Canadian Cataloguing in Publication Data

Godfrey, Ellen, 1942-
  Georgia disappeared

ISBN 0-14-023078-5

I. Title.

PS8563.O34G46 1992   C813'.54   C90-095635-6
PR9199.3.G64G46 1992

Lyrics to "Georgia On My Mind" by Hoagy Carmichael and Stuart Gorrell.
Copyright 1930 by Peer Internation Corporation. Copyright renewed
assigned to Peermusic Ltd. All rights in Canada controlled by Peer
International (Canada) Ltd.

In Memoriam

George Eliot, George Sand and Marian Halcombe

Good Women

Georgia, Georgia, the whole day through
Just an old sweet song
Keeps Georgia on my mind.

Georgia, Georgia, a song of you
Comes as sweet and clear
As moonlight through the pines.

Other arms reach out to me,
Other eyes smile tenderly,
Still in peaceful dreams I see
The road leads back to you.

I say Georgia, Georgia, no peace I find
Just an old, sweet song
Keeps Georgia on my mind.

from "Georgia On My Mind"
as sung by Ray Charles

CHAPTER 1

Everyone at the party was talking about the disappearance of Georgia Arnott. It was the first Jane had heard of it. She had been away for the past two weeks on business. And although Georgia and Jane had drifted apart over the last few years, Georgia remained dear to Jane; hearing of her disappearance was a terrible shock.

It was a very large party. There were perhaps a hundred people spread out over the lawns and gardens of the Caledon estate of Malcolm Morton. There were people drinking in small groups, standing under the big striped awning, clustered around the bar. There were people swimming in the pool; there were people playing badminton. There was a group, the women barefoot, playing croquet on a smooth patch of turf that ran along the side of the house down to the small, still lake where the cultivated lawns gave way to white rail-fenced horse pasture.

The warm June sun shone down on the grass, but Jane found the light peculiar. The sky had a grey tinge and the air was still, warm and lifeless.

1

Flies buzzed around the tables spread with food, settled on the guests playing croquet; there was one buzzing now around Simon Arnott, resting for a moment on his forehead, where there was a faint gloss of sweat. Jane leaned over to brush it off. Simon, languid, his eyes closed, seemed not to notice the gesture.

Simon was stretched out on a Cape Cod chair, his arms folded protectively over his chest, his glass of beer on the broad arm of his chair untouched and flat. In the bright sunlight Jane could see the lines on his face; she thought they looked deeper than when she'd last seen him—before Georgia disappeared. It was a long handsome face, with a bony, well-shaped prominent nose, strong narrow chin, slightly cleft, and thinning fair hair, artfully cut and blow-dried. Simon ran a powerful and successful advertising agency and was an important *éminence grise* and bagman to one of Canada's two governing political parties. He had the kind of face that looked good on television or in front of a group of insecure clients. Normally he looked strong, sincere and trustworthy. And normally, Jane thought, he looked handsome, but not today.

"Well, I guess I agree with you," Jane said, picking up the conversation. "Under ordinary circumstances Georgia wasn't likely to have taken off like that, of her own free-will, without telling anyone. But . . . maybe . . . if someone needed her and asked her to keep it a secret?"

"It's impossible, Jane," Simon said, without opening his eyes, his usually expressive voice flat. "You know Georgia. You know her sense of responsibility, how reliable and conscientious she was. She would never leave me without a note; she'd know I'd be worried to death about her. She wouldn't let Malcolm down. He trusted her, put her in charge of the Crystal Project when he took over Prospero. And she'd never leave her team at Prospero, not right now when so much depends on their finishing the project. There's millions of dollars and lots of jobs riding on Crystal's coming out on time. There's just no way on God's green earth that Georgia would walk out on that."

"Well, maybe the worry, the stress over—"

"You can say that, Jane, but Georgia wasn't worried. She was confident. She said things were going well, that they were ahead of schedule, that Crystal was looking sensational."

"That's right," said a voice behind Jane. She turned to see their host, Malcolm Morton, smiling down on them. Unlike Simon, who was elegantly dressed in pleated cream-white silk trousers and Italian woven shoes, Malcolm looked casual in an easy, relaxed way. He was a tall, strongly built man in his early fifties, thickening around the waist. His dark hair, which was receding on top, was cut very short. He had thick, unruly dark brows and small black eyes, whose full effect was rarely noticeable unless he looked directly at you. He wore immaculately pressed faded cotton trousers and old, worn, shapeless deck shoes without socks.

He sat down on the grass.

"Hello, Jane," he said, smiling politely at her. Then he turned his attention to Simon. "Si, I came to talk to you about Georgia, to see if you've heard anything, had any new ideas. It's been two weeks now—we can't go on like this much longer. We're going to have to come to some decisions pretty soon. You can understand that."

Simon opened his eyes and looked at Malcolm for a moment. "No," he said. "I haven't heard anything. You ought to know I'd tell you right away if I did."

"Okay, okay," Malcolm said, giving Jane a slight smile of complicity. "I'm concerned about her too, you know."

Jane returned the smile. Malcolm Morton was a person she wanted to know better—for business reasons. As an executive recruiter, Jane needed to cultivate the people who could use her firm's services. Morton was a financial power in Toronto—a man who invested in high-tech companies, building up small ones, rescuing sick ones, refinancing them, taking small private companies public. He was someone who could be an entrée into just the kind of business she specialized in, widening her contacts and opening up new opportunities for her. Jane's background was in computer software. Her boss counted on her to cover that side of the business and to bring in clients like Malcolm Morton.

"Sorry to jump on you like that, Malcolm," Simon said. "Probably I shouldn't have come. Everybody at the party has asked me about Georgia and it's driving me crazy. But staying home worrying has been getting to me, too. . . . Anyway, I've run out of polite ways to say: Don't look at me, I don't know where the hell she is!"

His voice rose at the end of the sentence, and Jane and Malcolm exchanged glances.

"I don't blame you for being upset about it," Jane said, putting her hand gently on Simon's for a moment. "I can imagine how hard it is on you. But a lot of people love Georgia. And, of course, they're worried."

"Yes," Malcolm said, "and a lot of people depend on her too. It's incomprehensible. Where are the police in all this? Are you getting all the support you should? If you need any help. . . ."

Simon sighed. "I have talked to everybody in the department, on up to the attorney general of the province. Believe me, they're doing everything they can. And there's just no trace of her. None." He sat up in the chair and looked forward, off into the distance, beyond Jane and Malcolm. His voice was very soft, almost inaudible. "I know people are saying she must be dead, but I just can't believe it, I won't believe it. If she'd been in an accident, surely we'd have heard something by now. But the police say the most likely thing is that she took off on her own for some reason. . . . They say maybe there was a side to her I didn't know, that our friends didn't know, a hidden side . . . that I should be prepared for that. They say it happens all the time; strange things come out when people disappear. I suppose that's true, but I just can't believe they're right about Georgia."

"I don't believe it either," Jane said. "Not for one moment. The police only talk that way because they didn't know Georgia."

Simon turned to Jane and smiled at her, a small

sad smile that was just a movement of the lips. "That's what I've been telling the police, but I don't think they believe me. But you know her, Jane. If Georgia was going to take off, for any reason, she'd never do it like that—at a party." His voice cracked slightly, "It's ridiculous what they're suggesting. At Pat's party she was her usual self. She talked to people, she ate, she drank, then . . . she was gone. Without saying goodbye, without saying anything to anybody. It doesn't make any sense! She never arrived home. She just disappeared. All she had were the clothes she was wearing: a silk dress, high heels, a light coat. Her regular purse, with a few hundred dollars and her credit cards. Strange way to run away, isn't it? She didn't take any money out of our account; she hasn't used her credit cards since. If she left under her own free-will, she made it look like she was snatched. And let me tell you—that's not Georgia. You were her friend, Jane, you know that."

"Yes, I know that."

"I know it, too," Malcolm said. "It's sure as hell puzzling, and I don't know what to say. Except that we're going to have to do something. The development team can't go on much longer without a team leader. And how do you find someone for a job like that, for an indefinite period? It's one hell of a mess."

Simon looked at Malcolm resentfully, and Jane could see that he thought Malcolm's business concerns were not the problem. "Maybe I can help," she said. "After all, that's what I do, you know— find people."

"Find people!" Simon said, sitting up and looking directly at Jane. "That's it! Why don't I hire you to find Georgia? You knew her, you know her friends. I'd pay so you could take the time to—"

"Hey, wait a minute," Jane said, laughing. "Not find missing people, I meant I find people for jobs. You know that, Simon." She stretched out her legs in front of her, leaning back in her chair, and glanced quickly at Malcolm to see if she still had his attention, and if he looked as if he might go for her idea of finding a temporary replacement for Georgia. She saw he was looking at her legs.

It was at this unpropitious moment that Tom came up to them. Jane looked up, saw him approaching, saw the way he was looking at the three of them. She could imagine what the scene looked like to him: she, leaning back, her legs stretched out in front of her, both men leaning towards her attentively. She tensed, her smile disappearing, dreading what was going to happen.

"Jane!" Tom said as he joined them. "So there you are. I was looking everywhere for you." Tom smiled at Malcolm and Simon and greeted them politely; they returned the greeting. But it was obvious that he was angry, and Jane, always combative when she felt threatened, felt her own irritation rising to meet his. How little it took to arouse his jealousy. Now there was going to be a nasty scene when they got home. She felt a trickle of fear, which made her angry at herself. Why do I let him frighten me? she thought. What am I afraid of? Am I cowardly because I think he'll hurt me and I'm not strong enough to defend myself?

That's ridiculous; Tom would never take it out on me. But she couldn't help thinking of the way, when he was in a rage, he would throw things across the room—a lamp, an ashtray. Of course, she told herself, be fair, that doesn't happen very often.

"Can I talk to you a minute, Jane?" he said.

She excused herself and they walked away from Simon and Malcolm. As soon as they were out of earshot, Tom said, "I'm ready to go home. Are you coming?"

"Oh Tom, they haven't even had the boat race yet. I want to stay for that. And anyway, it would be rude to leave so early."

He didn't say anything. He just looked at her, his face angry, his lips narrow and set.

Jane heard her voice rising, getting thinner, slightly squeaky. "And I think Malcolm may have a job for me. I'd like to stay a while longer and see if I can talk him into it."

"Talk him into it," Tom repeated, his tone sarcastic. "Is that what you were doing when you were displaying your legs to him?"

"I don't appreciate that," Jane said. "I think if you want to go home, you should. I'll find someone to give me a ride when I'm ready to leave."

He turned away and walked off towards the house. Jane watched him go, her fear of his anger changing to answering anger. What right does he have to treat me like that? she thought. I don't have to put up with it. I'm not going to put up with it. As she walked back towards Simon and Malcolm, who were watching her and had probably watched the quarrel, familiar words started repeating themselves in her head: "What's love got to do with it?"

Nothing, she told herself angrily, not a damn thing.

CHAPTER 2

The sky arched like a flat dull blue bowl. In the heat of late afternoon, a faint greyish haze was still hovering over the horizon. People were slowly converging on the small lake in twos and threes.

"My kids started this," Malcolm was saying to Jane as they approached the lake. "I bet it's twenty years ago now. The Curious George Boat Race." Jane remembered the children's book about Curious George. She had read those books to her own children; Curious George turning all his paper-route newspapers into sailing boats had been one of their favourites. She remembered that her ex-husband had not approved of the stories—of the feckless little monkey getting into trouble. Perhaps being Swiss, he thought disorderly triumphs were unsuitable. In any case, once he took the children, one of the few things she had been able to do for them that he could not was read them *Curious George*. She pushed the thought of her children, now virtually lost to her, out of her mind.

Malcolm was explaining the rules of the boat

race to the people gathered around. The boats had to be made of paper only. Glue was allowed. The paper could be treated—say with varnish. It could be twisted, bent, heated, cut, whatever. But fundamentally, the boats must be made only of paper.

Most of the competitors were men. A few were the guests' teenage boys. Over the years Malcolm's midsummer party boat race had become an institution, the boats increasingly ornate. Children and amateurs no longer competed.

"Come and meet the key people in the Crystal development group," Malcolm said to Jane, taking her elbow in a firm grasp and steering her through the spectators towards the far end of the lake. His touch, as he took her arm, seemed almost like a caress. Jane looked at him sideways, but he was looking around at his guests with a bland, friendly look and she thought perhaps she had imagined it. "They're very interesting people. If you're going to find a replacement for Georgia, it will be good for you to have met them."

Malcolm led Jane towards three people unpacking computer boxes, which had been stacked between the gnarled roots of a big, old willow close to the edge of the lake. It was a very small lake, more like a large pond, very still, with dense thickets of reeds growing on the far side and muddy banks. Along a small section of the shore an artificial beach had been created. It was here that most of the spectators had congregated, while the contestants were grouped along a stretch of the shore marked off with red flags. Just beyond this was the willow, its dark green boughs reaching almost to the ground.

Malcolm introduced Jane. "Jane, I'd like you to meet the Crystal team: Ivor Turlefsky, Red Kieran and Catherine Brooks." Jane shook each of their hands in turn. They all appeared to be in their early to mid-thirties—Jane's age, in fact—or perhaps a few years younger. Ivor was rather pasty looking, smallish, with a neat black beard and a large soft belly. Red was taller, stocky, with a frowzy reddish beard, balding with a freckled pate and soft, vulnerable-looking hazel eyes. Catherine was slender, dressed in a jumpsuit with pockets and zippers everywhere. Her face was nondescript, her expression repressed. Each in turn eyed Jane with what seemed to her a complete lack of interest. "Nice to meet you," Ivor said, "but we haven't got time for idle chit-chat now, Malcolm. We're going to blow them away. Wait until you see our fleet."

They were unpacking beautiful, delicate little boats, like origami. They had rubbery-looking paper keels and gunnels, and great windmill-like sails made of what appeared to be rice-paper. "These things will turn in the slightest wind . . . any wind at all and we'll blow the competition out of the water."

"But there isn't any wind—none," Jane said.

Ivor gave her a condescending look. "Just wait. It's under control."

"Maybe we should have tested them on windless days, Ivor," Red said. "You had Catherine and me working to protect them against too much wind."

"Not to worry. Like I said, it's all under control."

They were all tense. They were fitting the boats together, taking small bits out of their boxes. Each boat section was wrapped carefully in tissue and buried in Styrofoam packing peanuts. "We're gonna win this, you'll see. . . ." Ivor muttered.

Jane laughed. "Hey, guys, it's only a game."

They all turned and glared at her. "Okay, okay." She held up her hands in apology and stifled her amusement. "What's the prize this year, Malcolm?"

He smiled. "The same as always, the same as it's been every year, a little stuffed Curious George. Maybe that's why the competition has heated up. They're collectors' items now, you know. We have them made specially."

The three contestants had turned their backs on Jane and Malcolm and were protecting their boats from view as they completed their final assembly. Red turned to Jane and said somewhat apologetically, "Excuse us, but we have to watch out for industrial espionage."

As they walked back towards the other spectators, Jane said, "I think he was almost serious about that."

Malcolm was silent for a moment. "Oh, he was serious, all right. Those three are all fighters. That's one reason why I hired them in the first place. They're hostile and hard to manage, too. But they're brilliant, absolutely brilliant. This new product we're launching, they foresaw the market a couple of years ahead of everybody else and they did some extraordinary work to make it happen. A rare combination: strategic vision, the ability to plan and follow through. With Georgia to keep them under control, they were real world beaters. But now . . . I don't know. They seem pretty edgy to me. And I don't think it's just the boat race."

The race was being organized by a group of teenagers. Now one of them stood on a garden chair and blew a blast on a trumpet. The competitors launched their boats.

It was then that Jane and Malcolm saw that Ivor was taking out of one of his boxes a gigantic paper bellows. He sited along a surveyor's transit, lined it up and began blowing his own boat across the water. Catherine and Red looked astonished; soon all the guests were in an uproar. And Ivor's boat, outdistancing the others, sailed across the pond accompanied by his own triumphant shouts, mingled with cries from others of "foul," "cheat," and general laughter.

Malcolm, of course, was appealed to. Ivor came up, triumphant, holding aloft the winning boat, surrounded by his competitors claiming that he didn't deserve his victory.

Malcolm held up his hand for silence, quieting the crowd of guests to a low murmur. Then he carefully inspected the winning boat and the bellows. "In the opinion of your august and unbiased judge," Malcolm announced, "both the boat and the bellows are made of eligible materials. The winners are . . ."

There were shouts—"No! Cheat! Recount! Foul! Disqualify yourself, Malcolm!"

But Malcolm continued, "Ivor, Red and Catherine!"

Some of the guests now good-naturedly gathered around to congratulate the winners and inspect the design of the winning boat and the bellows. Others drifted off back towards the food and drink, the pool and the badminton and croquet games. A few of the competitors tried to argue with Malcolm, but he refused to engage and they, too, abandoned their complaints and returned to the party. Jane turned to look at the Crystal team, who were now packing up their boats. She heard a voice behind her: "I don't think it was fair. Do you, Jane?"

It was Simon, his hands in his pockets, standing beside her also studying the winners. "They're ruthless sons of bitches, those three. Georgia put up with a lot from them. This is typical, bloody typical."

Jane was surprised by his hostility. "Come on, Simon, it's only a game."

"No, Jane, you don't understand. There are people who play fair and people who don't. Those three don't. I always suspected it and this proves it."

Jane wasn't sure things were that simple. "Maybe all it proves is that they play to win."

"We all play to win. But I don't like people who step over the line to do it—that's all I'm saying."

Jane was silent, trying to decide what she thought about Ivor's tactics. He obviously hadn't told Red and Catherine of his plans, but they had not complained and had shared the credit. And she thought, too, that if Simon could count on knowing where the line of fairness was, he must be a pretty remarkable man. Especially in his profession. Knowing Simon, she did not believe he actually gave much thought to such matters. Whereas Georgia . . .

As if reading her thoughts, he said, "That's one of the things that makes Georgia so special. She has such clear vision, and she tries so hard to do what's right."

He turned to Jane. "I've had enough, Jane, I'm going home. I saw Tom leave. Do you need a lift?"

"Well, I was hoping to talk to Malcolm. . . ."

"Let me take you home, Jane. I want to talk to you about your looking for Georgia. Seeing that boat race—what if Georgia got in the way of those three at Prospero? And look how Malcolm Morton backed them."

"Well, I don't blame you for being worried. But, why me? If the police aren't the answer, surely there's someone who would be more help to you than me."

"I doubt that, Jane. Whoever I would find, they wouldn't understand about Georgia, they wouldn't be likely to understand Georgia's working world and they'd never have your insight into the people in Georgia's life. Look, I'm just asking you to discuss it with me, that's all. You love Georgia. She's a friend of yours. She often speaks of you as someone she really cares about. Please, Jane."

Jane felt good to hear that Georgia had spoken well of her, because Georgia was someone she loved very much. "All right," she said. What else was there to say?

"All right," she repeated. "Let's talk about it."

CHAPTER 3

Inside Simon's BMW Jane felt stiflingly hot. He had parked it locked, with all the windows up; now they opened them to let the heat escape. Too much alcohol, the unsatisfying party food, her limp clothes, the thin film of sweat on her body left her feeling irritable and tired.

Once off the side-roads and on to Highway 427, they found themselves in bumper-to-bumper traffic. They sat silent, but as the air-conditioning cooled their skin and the Mozart on the stereo calmed them, they began to talk. "I want you to help me find Georgia," Simon said to Jane. "I need you to help me."

Jane turned to look at Simon. His sad, pale blue eyes were heavy lidded with fatigue. The sun, low in the sky, flooded the car from the west, showing up dark circles under his eyes, the tense set of his shoulders. His voice was gentle, persuasive. "When we were talking, back there at the party, I remembered what Georgia said about you, how smart you are about people, how intuitive. How you're someone she can trust, no matter what."

17

"Georgia always overestimates me," Jane said uneasily. "You don't want to take that too seriously. And anyway, my boss would never let me."

"Why not, if I offer to pay you? It's a job. It's finding someone. I'm a business client, aren't I?"

Why not? Jane thought. Because it usually seemed that whatever she wanted, Eddie Orloff didn't? He certainly didn't trust her to do a decent job and seemed constantly surprised at her successes. Was it because he had been pressured by a satisfied client to promote her from researcher to associate, against his wish? What was it that caused Eddie to be so antagonistic to her? Who knew with Eddie Orloff.

"I don't know why not," Jane said. "But I know he won't go for it. That's all. He probably won't approve of my replacing Georgia with a person on contract either. He doesn't like that kind of business."

"But considering how big Morton is, he could hardly say no, could he?" Simon asked, taking his eyes off the road. They were stalled at one of the major intersections along Highway 427. They had hardly gone five miles in the last half-hour; the light was beginning to fade; it was close to nine o'clock; and Jane envied the few cars that flashed by going north, out of the city, their headlights dull in the twilight.

"Well, I guess it wouldn't hurt to try to convince him," Jane said, thinking that it probably would hurt. "And maybe, I could somehow make looking for Georgia part of the deal of working for Malcolm and finding her replacement, though at the moment I can't think how I would tie it in."

"You'll think of something," Simon said. It was half a plea, half a command. His voice rose, "I can't stand this. I can't stand the not knowing!"

Simon's anguish seemed to fill the car, to draw her in, as if it called to a kind of loneliness inside her that she had thought was no longer there since she and Tom had become lovers.

The traffic began to move again and there was silence between them as Simon manoeuvred, passing cars, pushing into the right lane, slowly gaining on the pace of traffic.

"But," Jane said softly, tentatively, "what if, what if you find out something that's worse than not knowing?"

"I won't. There's nothing worse." He turned towards her, taking his eyes away from the traffic again. "How are you and Tom?"

"We're fine," Jane said, wondering what she had said that had made him think of Tom.

"Any luck in your lawsuit to get access to your kids?"

"I'd rather not talk about that," Jane said.

"Sorry, but if there is anything I can do to help. . . ."

"There's nothing anybody can do."

They were both silent and Simon concentrated on his driving. Jane tried to resist thinking of her battle with her ex-husband over their children. She wanted them back. It was unbearable to be without them. After years of believing he had the right to raise them, because he had more to offer them and because to fight over them might harm them, she had changed her mind. But it seemed that way in court; he had the advantages of money and time. Now he had sent them to Switzerland for the summer, to spend the long holiday with his parents there, and, according to him, to polish their French. The two boys had wanted to go. Why wouldn't they? To be with her would be to spend a summer in her hot Rosedale apartment, with her working long hours. So, as Bernie pointed out, she wouldn't have that much time to spend with them in any case. He always seemed to be in a position to offer the children something better than she could. Surely money shouldn't be the deciding factor. But of course there was more to it than that, she thought. Bernie and his new wife loved the boys. They were devoted to them, to the idea of family, in a way that found no parallel in Jane's difficult, fragmented life.

Jane turned towards Simon, noticing how his hands gripped the wheel, and noticing at the same time the clean, soft leather of the car's interior, beautifully cared for, like all of Simon's possessions.

"Simon, tell me exactly what happened when Georgia disappeared."

"I told you already. That's it—there's nothing more to tell. She left the party. She vanished. Ask anyone, ask Ivor or Red, they were there. Ask Pat Hornsby, it was her party. But look, only one thing matters in all this. You know Georgia—the kind of woman she is. Extraordinary, right?"

Jane nodded, thinking about Georgia.

"I love her, we love each other. If there's anyone

in this whole world whom a person could be sure of, of their being truly loyal and good, it's Georgia. I know she did not just take off like that. She did not leave of her own free-will. And no one, no one could have reason to harm her. I can't help but think that maybe something terrible has happened, or maybe, is happening, to her."

"But, the police—"

"Forget the police! Two weeks and they haven't found out a thing. You're the right person to find Georgia. I need your help, Jane. Please."

Jane shook her head. What he was asking was absurd, impossible. But when she opened her mouth to tell him so, she heard herself saying, "Yes, of course I'll try. I'll try my best."

CHAPTER 4

Jane knew as soon as she saw Tom's glowering face at the door that she would have done better to have asked Simon to take her back to her own apartment. But she and Tom usually spent their weekends together. She looked forward to it all week. She had come to his place Friday after work and, now, her hair dryer, cosmetics, weekend clothes, everything—even her laundry—was at his place. It had seemed simplest to go back there as planned and get the inevitable fight over so that they could clear the air and have a pleasant Sunday together.

"What were you and Simon talking about in the driveway for so long?" he said.

"Could you at least wait until I'm inside before you start badgering me?" She was exhausted and she knew she didn't look good. Her cotton skirt and blouse were badly creased and there was a grass stain on her white espadrilles. Her hair had gone limp. Her make-up, she was sure, was gone and her skin felt greasy and dusty. A few minutes ago, saying good night to Simon, she had seen admiration in his eyes when he looked at her, and she had enjoyed the feeling that she was an attractive woman.

"It's ten o'clock," Tom said. "I've been home since five. The party was for lunch, not dinner."

Jane walked into the living-room and flopped on to the sofa. "Oh, give me a break. It's weekend cottage traffic. It took us three hours to drive twenty miles."

"Right." He sat down opposite her, stared at her for a moment. She looked back at him, her tiredness overcoming her anger at his pettiness, his quick jealousy, which she always found so inexplicable. Was it because he thought she was an unusually beautiful woman, so that any man she spent time with would want her? He must know that that wasn't so, but if that were the problem, maybe she should be flattered. Still she thought it unlikely. She thought Tom was good-looking, but that didn't make her jealous. Even though she knew there had been many women in his life before her, she rarely thought about them. What difference could his past make to their life together?

He had been married, his wife had left him for someone else, and he had, as he put it, "played the field" before he and Jane had become lovers, agreeing to see only each other. It was an agreement that had been very important to Tom and that Jane had welcomed, but it seemed to have heightened rather than diminished his irrational jealousy. Maybe he thinks I'm sending out signals to other men, she thought.

"I wasn't flirting with Simon," Jane said, feeling sorry that she had hurt him without knowing how or why. "He is so worried about Georgia. We talked about that."

"She'll turn up," Tom said. His tone was slightly less frigid. "She's probably left him for someone else. Gone off for a few weeks to think things through. Figure out how to tell him."

"That's not like Georgia. I don't believe it."

"Okay, if you say so. Anyway, I've known Simon a long time. I'm sure he can handle it." Tom was vice-president of sales for a major computer company, he had worked with Simon's agency from time to time. "Simon likes you," he said. "I could see it."

"Sure, of course he likes me. And I like him. Right now we're both worried about Georgia. And that's all. Why do you do this, Tom? Why do you treat me like this? I've never given you any reason. You knew me before we started living together. Was I that easy? That available? Did I ever give you reason to suspect that I would hop into bed with any man who smiled at me?"

He looked at her for a moment, his brows drawn together, then walked over to her, sat down beside her, put his arms around her and began kissing her gently on the neck.

"Hey, you don't want to do that," Jane said. "I'm all sweaty."

"I'm sorry, Jane. This thing just comes over me and I think every man must want you as I do. I think of all the women I meet who come on to every guy and then I just get scared that I am going to lose you."

She put her arms around him, loving this side of him, his gentleness, his willingness to apologize.

"What you saw at the party—it was business with Malcolm, it was friendship with Simon. All we talked about was Georgia. Simon wants me to try to find her. At first I said no, the idea seems so ridiculous. But he's convinced himself I can help, so I said I'd give it a try."

Tom pulled away from her. "No! Absolutely not. That's crazy. Out of the question."

"Tom," Jane said, turning to him, running her hand lovingly over his cheek, "Georgia is my friend."

"Orloff will never agree to it."

She sighed. "That's what I think too. I'll have to think of some way to convince him, or trick him, or something. It's not going to be easy. Why couldn't I have a nice reasonable boss?"

"Orloff's not so bad," Tom said. "I've told you that before. At least you know where you are with him."

"I guess we've agreed to disagree about him. If you could see the way he treats me, you'd know I'm right; he's out to get me and I have to watch my back all the time with him."

"I'll watch your back for you, Jane," Tom said, taking her into his arms and lovingly caressing her. She nestled close to him, glad for his presence, and glad that with him she was able to forget her problems and feel safe.

CHAPTER 5

Jane had a plan. But, as usually happened, Eddie Orloff outwitted her.

He was sitting behind his gleaming French mahogany campaign-style desk, the brass corner fittings reflecting the light from the window as if they were gold. Behind him she could see down on to Bay Street and into the windows of the building across the street, into offices, which looked like brightly coloured stage sets.

Orloff was at his most genial. Usually he sent for Jane when he had an assignment for her he had been unable to convince the client would be better done by another associate. Or he might have decided that her knowledge of the computer industry, particularly software, made Jane the only reasonable choice for the client in question. Then, he was resentful, annoyed, sarcastic. But when Jane initiated the meeting herself, it could only be because she was beyond her depth, needed help and was obliged to turn to him, recognizing his experience and willing to pay the price of enduring his small cruelties to get it. Or because she wanted something from the firm, something he might find himself in the position of being able to refuse. Either of these two options were, Jane always thought, particularly pleasing to him.

In any case, this was how Jane explained to herself Orloff's shifting attitudes towards her. And now, looking at him, she saw how relaxed he was, sitting calmly in his elegant leather chair, fiddling with his fat Mont Blanc pen and smiling at her. She took a deep breath telling herself to relax, so that her voice would not take on that high, breathy squeak that she found so demeaning. She sat up as tall as she could so that she would not have to look up at him, but could try to meet him at eye-level.

"I think you'll be glad to hear, Eddie, that I had a good talk with Malcolm Morton at his Midsummer's Day party this weekend."

Orloff smiled, as if to say that he was surprised at her being invited at all, let alone having been given an opportunity to talk to the great Malcolm Morton. Then he gently tapped the rounded cap of his pen against his teeth to signal his impatience and his desire that she get to the point.

"Malcolm and I talked about my finding a replacement for Georgia Arnott. She's head of new products development at his company, Prospero."

"Prospero . . . Prospero? Let's see. . . . Isn't that the company that was on the rocks, new products late, ran out of cash, he bailed them out? General view is, they're going into the tank."

Jane gritted her teeth. "Yes, that's one way to describe it," she said. "But it's not going to go down. Malcolm hired Georgia Arnott to get a new product out the door. The prototype has impressed everybody in the industry. The trade papers and industry watchers are predicting great things. Now they're ahead of the schedule Georgia committed to when she joined Prospero. The new release is coming out this fall. They have big advance orders. Georgia has worked miracles and it's looking like a great turnaround. . . ."

"Right, right, now I remember the latest. People are saying that if this new software product is as good as first reports, the company will go like gangbusters and Morton will take it public and make a killing. So, why replace Georgia if she's God's gift?"

"The problem is she's disappeared. Of course, the hard part of her work is done, but getting from prototype through the last round of field testing and through product release is tough too. It's a critical time. They've got to stay on schedule. And they've got to find someone to hold the fort until Georgia turns up."

"What's supposed to have become of the lady?" Orloff said, pulling his lips back and running his pen top along his teeth. He looked, to Jane, like a wolf brushing his teeth.

"Nobody knows what's happened to her, but she's bound to turn up. It's so unlike her," Jane said.

"Unlike her? How so?"

"You'd have to know her," Jane said, hesitating. How to describe Georgia, how to describe the special qualities of Georgia to someone like Eddie.

She didn't know where to begin. "She's so . . . she'd just never let anyone down. Anyway," she hurried to add, "here's my idea. I know Orloff Associates doesn't place people on contract, for limited time periods, so I'm going to volunteer to fill in myself. I'm asking you for a leave to do that. I think that offer will really impress Morton. After all, no matter how good we or any of our competitors are, it would be impossible to find someone to hold down the fort as quickly as is needed. By offering to do that, we can offer him a service he won't find anywhere else. And, of course, at the same time I'm filling in and learning what kind of person is needed, I'll be looking for a replacement; I'll get someone lined up if Georgia can't come back."

He smiled his feral smile. "Right, so when the body turns up we'll be right there with the replacement, the competition won't even get a shot at it."

"Eddie!" Jane said, horrified by his words. "Nothing that bad has happened to her. There's no reason to think that."

"Okay, okay, have it your own way. Time will tell on that one. Pointless to argue it. But as for your idea. . . ."

Now Jane expected Orloff to tell her that the idea was outrageous, that Malcolm would never go for it and that she was completely unqualified to fill in for Georgia. But in this case, he'd make an exception to Orloff policy and let her try to sell Malcolm on the idea of finding someone on a temporary contract basis—someone qualified. Because he'd be tempted by the chance for Orloff

Associates to do business with Malcolm Morton, and by the potential for more business if Georgia's departure proved to be caused by a debilitating illness, a breakdown of some sort, or a serious personal problem. And this was what she was counting on his saying, because while she was working to fill the temporary position she would have time and opportunity to help Simon and look into Georgia's disappearance. But she feared if she suggested it, Orloff would refuse.

He would surely never agree to Jane's taking on a position in a client firm. It was unprofessional, unprecedented and just the kind of thing she knew he most abhorred. Jane was suggesting it as a red herring, and to give him something to reject so that he would go along with what she really wanted.

"I think it has real possibilities."

But, of course, why hadn't she seen it? She was playing right into his hands. He wanted to get rid of her, and she was giving him the ideal opportunity.

"As a service of Orloff Associates, of course," she said, trying to think how to backtrack, how to get out of it. But she did want to help Simon, wanted that very much. Wouldn't this plan, which she had meant only as a ruse, give her the best possible chance to find out what had happened to Georgia? Being right inside Prospero, she'd have an opportunity to find clues to Georgia's disappearance. And if Jane went there on behalf of Orloff, surely he couldn't refuse to take her back at Orloff Associates when Georgia returned, or needed replacing. But that wasn't the biggest problem. The biggest problems were one, she couldn't possibly do Georgia's job—Was that why Orloff had that grin of malicious delight?—and two, she had implied Malcolm Morton would go for it, when in fact he most likely wouldn't. Oh God.

"So it's settled then," said Orloff, standing up. He towered over Jane, who stood up quickly, feeling as she always did—belittled when he came close to her. He, over six feet tall, straight, supple; she, five-two, slightly pudgy, soft and indistinct in comparison. "I assume you wouldn't have come to me if Morton wasn't already onside, and of course, you'll be a caretaker, so you must think the job is mostly administrative. Despite what you've been saying, I assume you wouldn't have volunteered if there were any chance you could screw up Morton's business through inexperience or incompetence. That right?"

Jane smiled weakly.

"Naturally, we'll have to make sure Morton knows that the firm is not representing you as anything more than a caretaker. We don't want any liability for representing you as something you're not. But you'll have thought about all that. Let me see some paper on how you plan to handle all these issues, a release from Morton, that kind of thing."

"Well, I . . ."

"Glad to see you showing initiative here, Jane." This time there was no mistaking the mocking quality of his smile. "Of course, if you screw up, you'll be on your own. We wouldn't be able to cover you."

Jane's anxiety, as so often happened, now turned to anger, her anger to a rush of adrenaline and a feeling of power that she knew, from experience, often led her to venture beyond safe limits. "Of course," her voice was calm, her tone even contained a mocking note like a faint echo of Orloff's. "I wouldn't want it any other way. But if I pull it off, it would be only fair if I became a senior associate."

"Tregar, if you were a man, I'd have to say you had balls. As it is, let's just leave it at this—you screw up, you're on your own. You do well, we'll look at it. Now don't press me. We've played enough games for one afternoon."

"That's not acceptable."

"Well, little lady, I'll promise you this: when all this is over, you'll get what you deserve. You have my word on that."

CHAPTER 6

Malcolm Morton was the kind of man business people liked to boast about knowing. The principal in a very successful venture capital firm, he had, over the past decade, built a capital base of over $100 million. His deal-making skills were admired, and at the same time he was praised for his loyalty to his friends and for his integrity—a powerful combination. And now, having come out cash rich from the crash of October '87, and buoyed by the overheated Ontario economy, Morton was investing in high-technology companies, sitting on government advisory boards and being constantly quoted in the press.

Jane had met Malcolm Morton through her friendship with his ex-wife, Pat Hornby. She had also recruited executives for one of his companies, although she had not worked with him directly. But when Malcolm and Pat's marriage had broken up the previous year, Jane no longer had had any reason to see Malcolm. Her loyalties were with Pat, and she had listened with sympathy to her stories about how awful Malcolm had been. Of course, she wasn't sure she knew where the truth lay in all these stories, but who was she to judge a marriage?

Her own marriage breakup was still a painful mystery to her, but she knew it seemed perfectly clear to outsiders.

Her husband, a sophisticated wealthy man, had seen in Jane a young pretty woman, half his age, courted her, swept her off her feet, married her, sired two beautiful boys, kept her as long as she played the role of dutiful wife. Then, when she no longer would, he dumped her and took the children. And Bernie's wealth and arrogance tended to make people think he was the villain of the piece, especially since he had remarried immediately after the divorce. But his side of it? Sometimes, talking to her men friends, Jane got a whiff of the other—the man's side. And there were her strong feelings that somehow her own failures had played a large part in what had happened.

Now Jane had to see Malcolm Morton, to convince him to go along with her plan. He had agreed to meet with her to discuss her ideas, suggesting that since he could not fit her in during the week, she come up to his farm in Caledon on Sunday. Jane had accepted, despite the fact that she really needed a good long weekend with Tom to try to reassure him after their fight the previous Saturday.

She'd been worrying about the meeting with Morton all week. It would have been daunting in any case, and the fact that she had convinced him to see her under false pretences—finding a replacement for Georgia—made it worse.

She had spent part of the week doing research on Morton and his companies. By Wednesday, feeling more and more anxious about the upcoming encounter, she had called Pat Hornby and invited herself to Pat's place for the Saturday. She'd been frank with Pat, and told her that she wanted something from Malcolm and needed Pat's help to figure out how to get it. Pat had been nice about it, saying she was always glad to see Jane, why not come up on Saturday, spend the night, they could swim and drink and talk, and Pat would help any way she could.

So now, Jane was driving over the country roads, circling through the low green hills, past the white painted fences and rough-rail fences of Caledon horse country, past the stone gates of Malcolm Morton's house, along the Third Line, over the ruts in the dirt road, to Pat's.

Jane was remembering that Malcolm had been surprisingly good about the separation. Pat had loved the Caledon farm, where the couple had spent their weekends and as much of their summer as they could. So Malcolm had set off fifty acres of his two hundred and fifty, and given it to Pat as part of the settlement. He had also given Pat a generous cash settlement, so she was able to build a house with a pool and to have the property looked after during the week. A friendly separation, everyone said. That was really hard for Jane to understand. And though Pat had explained to Jane the reasons for her divorce, she had explained it differently each time.

Jane drove the Triumph over the grassy hill to

the house and parked alongside of it. Pat's house
was a long, low, glass and cedar-siding rectangle,
with a shake roof, and big fieldstone chimney on
one side. Sliding-glass doors along the back
opened out on to a cedar deck, with steps down to
the swimming pool. Beyond the pool, grass
stretched away for several acres, ending in a bush
of cedar, maple and birch. Everything was immac-
ulate, groomed, peaceful. Along the deck were
cushioned chaise longues and large clay pots filled
with cascading dark purple petunias. Pat was lying
on one of the chaises, watching as Jane climbed
out of her car, carrying her suitcase.

To Jane who felt tense, hot and grimy, after her
worrying week and long drive, the whole scene was
extraordinarily welcoming and calm: the bright
sunlight, the relaxed figure of her friend, the pool
sparkling and quivering in the sunlight. She threw
her bag down and collapsed with a sigh on to a
chair near Pat's. "Boy it's hot. I can't wait to jump
in the pool and wash the city away—wash everything away."

Pat smiled. She was a woman of about fifty, with
short, dark wavy hair streaked with grey, a plump
body and dark skin. She has a beautiful face, Jane
thought, watching as Pat sat up, took off her sunglasses, and swung her legs over the chair. Pat was
wearing a plain red tank suit and Jane could see
her large pendulous breasts, pressed down against
her rib-cage by the swimsuit. Pat smiled more
broadly as she caught Jane's glance.

"I know, I know," she said, "I've been gaining
four or five pounds a year since I went into book

publishing. It must be all the drinking and eating I do in the line of duty. I don't know how you keep your gorgeous figure." Pat ran her fingers through her dark hair and grinned at Jane. "One good thing—men seem to like my fat, so what the hell. Go on in and put on your suit, or skinny-dip if you like. No one's here but you and me. I left the latest lover in the city this weekend; I wanted to have some time alone to unwind."

"I'm sorry if—"

"Oops, that was tactless of me. Of course I didn't mean you, Jane, you're always welcome. I meant men, and holding my stomach in and wearing make-up, remembering not to fart, you know. And having to listen when I want to talk."

"Well, please feel free to let everything out with me around," Jane said. "I intend to unwind too. I'm going to go in and change. Be right back." She slid open the glass doors, enjoying the rush of cool air-conditioned air and the smooth feel of the red quarry tiles on her hot feet. The doors opened directly into a big living- dining-room kitchen, decorated with informal white rattan and stripped-pine furniture.

Jane went along to the end bedroom and threw her suitcase on the bed. She could hear the sounds of flies buzzing in the windows, and a few fly corpses lay on the window-sills. Other than this, the room had a pristine, barely lived-in air. Jane zipped open her case, hung up the cotton shirt and neatly pressed cotton trousers she had brought, took off her wrinkled shorts and T-shirt and changed into her swimsuit. Then she padded back along the corridor to the kitchen, searched until she found some mineral water, filled two glasses with ice water, and brought them both outside.

Pat was lying back again, her face, tilted up to the sun, glistening with sweat and sun-tan oil. Jane sat down next to her feeling her thighs stick to the stiff cotton duck of the chair cushion. "Boy, it's hot," Jane said. "I had the top off the car and I still feel like a sardine that's been sizzled in the tin."

Pat slid her sunglasses up over her head, turned to look at Jane, saw the drink and picked it up, saluting Jane. "Thanks, sardine. I needed this and was too lazy to get up for it." A pile of manuscripts lay on the deck around her chair. There were more boxes of them on a side-table.

"I thought you were too senior to read manuscripts," Jane said.

"Hah! You must have been thinking of somebody else. Everyone real in publishing reads manuscripts. We would probably waste away to wraiths without them. I think if I left work on Friday without thirty pounds of manuscripts in my right hand, I'd cant to the left and fall over. So, how have you been, Jane? And how's gorgeous Tom?"

"I'll tell you," Jane said. "Swim first." She walked over to the pool and, without testing the water, jumped feet first into the deep end. As she sank, she felt as if, for a moment, she had left her tensions and fears on the surface and had entered a cool, peaceful realm where she was weightless and free. The water shimmered blue green and ease flowed through her. Then her feet touched bottom and she was floating back up towards the surface. She broke through, tilted her head back, and felt the cold water against her scalp and the sun, bright, almost painful, in her eyes. It was very quiet. There was only the faint chinking noise of the water against the side of the pool, disturbed by her body. She swam a length, lazily, using her arms, kicking only once or twice, then pulled herself on to the side of the pool and squeezed the water out of her hair.

The water in the pool was rocking, thousands of tiny shallow cups filled with sunlight, jostling each other, flattening slowly, growing calmer. She kicked her feet, setting up new eddies that disturbed the growing calm and set everything quivering again.

Pat walked over and sat down beside her. She, too, kicked her feet into the water, and the two women watched as the pattern of wavelets intersected, broke upon each other and reformed.

"How have you been anyway?" Pat asked. She handed Jane a towel and Jane rubbed it over her hair, knowing she would have to rewash and wave it again the next morning, but that how she looked now didn't matter.

"How have I been?" Jane repeated. "Okay, I guess. I'm sort of living with Tom now. Or, at least, I spend most weekends with him."

Pat darted a look at Jane which Jane could not interpret and felt a sudden curious stab of fear. It was an anxious look, a look a mother might give a child who had just explained that she had decided to take up sky-diving.

Jane was fifteen years younger than Pat. They had met at the University of Toronto, where Pat had come to study after her kids were grown up. Jane, recently married to a sophisticated older man, had found herself with responsibilities and obligations that had often seemed overwhelming. She had been drawn to Pat who had exuded a kind of maternal warmth. Jane had always thought that this characteristic was part of the powerful attraction Pat seemed to exert on men: there were always a few around her and had been all the time she was married to Malcolm; more now that she was divorced. But Pat swore she would never marry again, that it was an unnatural state for her, that she'd have casual lovers until she got to the age when no one wanted her. Then, she'd said, she'd manage with pornography and her imagination. "I don't want the job of looking after a man," she'd said, "worrying about his fragile ego. No thank you. All they ever want to do is get married and then you end up carting their dry-cleaning, running their houses, entertaining their friends and having to act according to their idea of who they are. Forget it."

Now, watching Pat, Jane realized that part of the reason she had come here was to get some comfort and reassurance before her interview with Malcolm. That, as much as learning the inside story about Malcolm and about Georgia's disappearance. Yet, for some reason, she found herself talking to Pat about none of these things. Instead, she was telling Pat about her problems with Tom.

"I love him, I really do, but the trouble is he's irrationally jealous. It just blows up out of the blue, for no reason that I can figure out. He thinks every man who sees me wants me, that something is going on if I spend any time with a man. And you know, in my business, I spend almost all my working time with men. I've been completely faithful to him. I just don't get it."

Pat smiled, a knowing smile. "Completely faithful—what does that mean?"

"It means I haven't slept with anyone but him since we met," Jane said angrily. Then, looking at Pat's amused expression she said, "But it is strange: it's as if his jealousy and possessiveness are giving other men ideas. Before I began sleeping with Tom I went through a couple of years where I didn't want anybody and nobody wanted me. And now . . . it's like . . . wherever I go it seems that I meet someone and there's this spark. . . ."

"You're sending out signals. That's what it is."

"But why? If I am, and I don't think so, but if I am, why am I? I love Tom. It's as if his jealousy has made me a little . . . a little"—she waved her hand, not finding the word.

"Nuts," Pat said. "He's sending you mixed messages and he's driving you crazy, that's what it is."

Jane shook her head. "I don't understand what you mean. But anyway, I didn't come up here to talk about my love life. I want to hear about Malcolm. I need to know what makes him tick."

"Oh you do, do you. Well for that we need a drink. Don't move. I'll be right back."

Jane noticed that the sun's rays were longer and

slanting and there was a thickening quality in the light. She found her watch where she had put it on a little table beside her chair. Four o'clock. Pat came back with a bottle of wine in a terracotta wine bucket, two glasses, some cheese, grapes and crackers.

"Malcolm," she said. "Where to begin? Malcolm.
. . ."

"Malcolm," Jane said smiling. "Tell me about the man who has everything—the man you left."

"He's very complicated. A driven man. Loyal, in his way. He wasn't very good to me, you know, but if you were to ask him, he'd say the opposite—that he loved me very much, did everything for me. And I know he believes that. He can't understand why I left, though I know he tries. But I don't let it worry me. One thing Malcolm Morton will never have is a broken heart. He's put his heart in some kind of deep hidden place and I don't think anyone is ever going to get anywhere near it. Still, you have to give him credit. His parents were horrible people. His sisters and brothers have all destroyed themselves. Considering everything, Malcolm is very sane."

"But why did you leave him, if . . . ?" It was a question Jane had asked Pat before and never gotten the same answer twice. Once the answer had been that it was because Pat had fallen in love with someone else. Another version was that Malcolm spent so much time on his business activities that their marriage was virtually non-existent anyway. This time Pat said, "Maybe because I got tired of loving him, that's all. It's very fatiguing—loving—

you know. You get to my age, you get tired of it."

"I don't know what you're talking about," Jane said.

Pat got up and began walking restlessly back and forth along the length of the pool. "What to tell you. . . . I don't know what to tell you," she said, half talking to herself.

"My reason for seeing Malcolm," Jane said, "is partly business, as I told you on the telephone on Wednesday, but also it's kind of mixed up with Georgia Arnott's disappearance."

"Georgia? What does Malcolm know about that?"

"It's complicated." Jane explained about her conversation with Simon, how worried she was about him, how sorry for him she felt, how she wanted to help if she could. And about her plot to trick Orloff into letting her and how it had backfired.

"Kind of messy," Pat said, looking worried.

"Georgia's disappearance has put Malcolm's company, Prospero, on the spot and, of course, he'll need to do something about it. But that's a long way from enough to convince him that I could take her place. I've never run a software development team. It's ridiculous to think—"

"No, there you're wrong. It's the kind of thing Malcolm likes to do: find bright people and throw them into new things. He's always doing that. No, I think you'll be surprised. If you just act like you know you can do it and if he doesn't have any better idea, he might go for it. Even if he's looking for something better, he might let you have a try while he looks. No, that's not the problem, that's not what's worrying me."

"Worrying you?"

Pat stopped her pacing and stood looking down at Jane for a moment. Then she sat down on the end of Jane's chaise longue. Jane moved her legs, making room for Pat. "Yes," Pat said. "I don't want you to do this."

"Do what? Take Georgia's place?"

"That's right, Jane. Look what happened to Georgia. She disappeared. No one knows where. But you and I know she didn't leave willingly. That's not something Georgia would do when people were counting on her. And there's more. I know enough to know that it wouldn't be a good idea for you to try to find out what happened to Georgia." Pat leaned forward, her dark eyes looking at Jane with affection and concern.

"I don't understand you," Jane said. "What possible harm could come from trying to find out what happened?"

"Plenty of harm could come from it—to you. Especially to you. Please, forget it, Jane."

Jane found herself getting frightened and then angry. "Why? Why should I? Give me one good reason."

Pat ran her fingers through her hair, then down over her forehead. Then she put her hand around her neck as if to smooth out the skin where age was beginning to loosen it. "Please, trust me, Jane. What you're thinking of doing, it's a big mistake. It could be very dangerous for you."

"Oh come on. That's the most ridiculous thing

I've ever heard. Just stop talking like that, Pat. I won't listen to it. Simon is at his wit's end. And if I can help, I'm going to. So what if I find out things about Georgia or Prospero or whatever? Isn't it always better in the end to know the truth? Isn't it?"

"No, Jane," Pat said sadly, getting up and walking back to her chair, her expression sombre.

Jane, remembering her conversation with Simon, where she had taken the other side, thought for an instant how odd it was that she thought others might be hurt by the truth, but, for her, it could only be liberating. "Well, you're out of luck, Pat," she said. "Because whether you help or not, I'm going to find out what happened to Georgia, if I can."

"I'm sorry to hear that," Pat said. She lay back on her chair, turned her face up to the sun and closed her eyes. Jane followed her example and let the warmth of the sun still her doubts.

CHAPTER 7

Her car bounced and creaked as Jane wheeled it over the grassy track that led down the slope from Pat's house, and on to the gravel side-road leading to Malcolm's.

In her rear-view mirror she saw a plume of grey-brown dust behind her, but ahead the road gleamed in the late morning light. Reflections off the holes and ruts appeared to be pools of water, but when she approached them they were only mirages.

Instead of planning her strategy for the meeting, Jane was worrying about how she was dressed. Her khaki trousers were already creasing in the heat of the car and her white polo shirt was sticking to her back. Sometimes she truly believed she created an illusion of power with the right clothes: bulky suits, high heels, large square gold earrings. But dressed like this . . . Malcolm would, most likely, think of her as a cute little thing, listen, smile, then dismiss her. Of course she could probably get his attention by flirting, but that would be the wrong sort of attention and would do her more harm than good.

She realized she had gone past his gateposts and turned in at the next lane. She backed out and retraced her path. The dust the car had stirred up sifted over her and settled on her hair, lips, eyes and the white shirt.

Malcolm's long driveway was paved with fine gravel. It twisted between beautiful old maples, past the lake, and led to the house. The house was a century-old brick farmhouse, with white trim and ornate gingerbread along the gables. It had been added to in back, but the front was authentic; it looked solid and assured. She parked the car in a circular parking area, in the shade of a large maple, wiped off her face and hands as best she could, and got out of the car.

As Jane approached along the bricked walk, which was lined with masses of white petunias, the front door opened and Malcolm came out. "Hello, hello," he said, smiling at her and shaking her hand with enthusiasm. "I appreciate your coming all the way up here on such a beautiful Sunday. Let's go around to the back and get something to drink. You must be hot from the drive."

She followed him around the side of the house to a patio that overlooked the sloping lawns dotted with maples, which cast their complex shadow patterns over the grass. One of the trees spread its boughs over part of the terrace, and under its shade a table was set with drinks and small sandwiches. "Lunch," he said.

Jane, who had eaten a late breakfast of toast and fruit with Pat, had no appetite. The two women had stayed up late gossiping and drinking. Pat had told Jane everything she knew about Georgia's disappearance, unwillingly, after drinking more than her share of the second bottle of wine. But Jane had learned nothing that explained Pat's curious reluctance to talk about Georgia, or Pat's obvious unhappiness over Jane's intent to look into her whereabouts. It was clear that there were many things Pat was not going to talk about. And what she did speak of seemed flat, as if it were a story recounted second hand by someone who hadn't been there. Yet it was at Pat's party that Georgia had disappeared. Surely Pat had thought about it, asked questions, relived it many times in her mind, looking for clues. Why had she told Jane so little?

"Have a sandwich," Malcolm said, pouring out mineral water for himself. Jane helped herself to ice and mineral water. She had hoped to have a chance to wash her hands and face. She felt hot and dirty, while Malcolm, in his white duck trousers, blue denim shirt and woven Italian loafers, looked impeccable.

"Relax and unwind," Malcolm said. "Did you drive up this morning? How long did it take you?"

"Actually, I came up yesterday and spent some time with Pat. I hadn't seen her in a long time."

He leaned back in his chair and looked past Jane, across the broad expanse of his property, and smiled a little. "Pat, how is she? How did she seem to you?"

"Oh, fine. We always have fun together. But we talked quite a bit about Georgia's disappearance, and that seemed to bother her."

"Did it? That's odd. They weren't that close, as far as I know."

"That's what I thought."

"Oh, well, Pat gets peculiar ideas sometimes. Then she's very stubborn and all the rational talk in the world doesn't seem to have any effect. And I'm not just saying that because she's my ex-wife. We're still good friends."

"Well, anyway," Jane said, "Georgia is missing and that's why I wanted to talk to you. Has Prospero found a replacement? How are they managing?"

Malcolm frowned. "As far as I can tell, the Prospero management has done nothing about the problem. Of course, things are still fluid. When I took over I fired the president and his three top managers. They were all worthless. They were spending money like they believed their own prospectuses." He laughed, and Jane heard in his laughter an artificiality and tenseness that the energy of his strong physical presence had hidden from her. "I've replaced them, of course, but the new men haven't really taken hold yet. They've let the Georgia problem drag on. Probably they think each day she's going to turn up. Of course, to do them justice, they have plenty of other problems on their plate. Coming in cold to a twenty-million dollar software company that's in big trouble is no piece of cake. Still, it's not good enough."

"I was hoping I could help."

"I'm hoping you could, too. Why don't you tell me what you have in mind?"

"Finding a replacement, of course," Jane said.

She twisted her legs around the chair legs and put both her hands around her water glass.

"You're not eating," Malcolm said. "Have a sandwich. Try those smoked salmon and cream cheese ones. The salmon is very good. We have it specially smoked. I'd like to know what you think of it." He took one of the sandwiches, put it on a square wooden plate and helped himself to vegetables from a platter of raw celery, carrots, cauliflower, zucchini and tomatoes. "The vegetables are all from our garden. We start them in the greenhouse; that's why we have them so early. No chemicals. You really should try some."

Jane took a carrot and bit down on it. The crunchy noise her teeth made was surprisingly loud.

"Well, how were you going to go about finding someone? It's a bit problematical when Georgia could show up any day. And then there's the confidentiality aspect of it all. Do we want a contract person working on that project? It's the major product of Prospero. I'd want whoever works on it to sign a non-competition agreement covering at least two years—maybe longer. And who is going to do that for a possibly brief term, if they're any good? It seems to me that's the central problem. How do you intend to get around that?"

Jane worried at her carrot, trying to take little nibbles rather than big, noisy bites. "I had a somewhat outrageous idea I thought might appeal to you," she said, making her voice as offhand as possible, though she thought from the way Malcolm was looking at her that she hadn't fooled him in the least—he knew how nervous she was. She untwisted her legs from the chair and stretched them out nonchalantly in front of her. One trouser leg, she noticed, had a very noticeable orange stain on it. Perhaps a rust mark from the iron chair leg. Damn!

"Let's hear it. Outrageous ideas are my favourite kind."

Jane was encouraged. Maybe Pat had been right. Malcolm liked to see himself as innovative, original, master of the surprising move.

"I thought I'd take it over while I looked for someone. Then there'd be no rush. And if Georgia turns up in the meantime, all the better."

"You!" Malcolm said, surprised out of his good manners. "What do you know about managing software development teams?"

"I specialized in computer science," Jane said. It was a lie. In fact, although she had taken almost as many computer science courses as someone going for a B.Sc., Jane had been a psychology major.

"But you've never done anything like this, have you?" he said looking at her closely, as if trying to understand what she was really thinking, what she could do. It was an intense, measuring look. Jane looked back at him, wishing she understood him better, wishing she knew what she could say to convince him.

"I need to think about that," he said. He stood up. "How would you like to see our horses? They're quite wonderful. Grab a sandwich and come on, I want to show you."

Jane followed him along a brick pathway that

led to a narrow gravel road. He slowed down so she could walk by his side, and she quickened her step to keep up with him.

She could feel the heat of the midday sun beating down on her hair and prickling the flesh on her arms. Along the roadway were maples and ash, but with the sun at its zenith they cast no shadow over the road itself.

They approached the stables, which were new but had been built of the same old rosy brick as the house. Beyond the stables was a paddock, and beyond this a large pasture with white rail fences and a row of old, untended apple trees at one end. They walked over to the paddock and Malcolm pointed to some horses that had just been brought back from being exercised and were being unsaddled.

"The best of the lot, by far, is that tall bay. Do you see?" He pointed to an ungainly looking bay, with one white foot and a manner of tossing his head up which seemed to be annoying the horse exerciser. They walked around the fence and leaned over. "That's Risk Taker," Malcolm said. "We think he's going to win a lot of races for us. He thinks so too. Look at him." The horse edged away from the old man who was running his hands along his legs, checking him over. Malcolm and Jane entered the paddock and walked over to the horse, admiring him. Jane stroked the horse's nose, and Risk Taker butted her shoulder with an impatient, arrogant movement.

Without thinking, she said, "Oh, how I'd love to ride him!" She looked up at Malcolm half smiling, then her smile faded and their eyes locked for a moment. Jane dropped her eyes, smiled again, then took the reins from the surprised groom, slid her foot into the stirrup and swung her leg over the horse's back. The groom started to protest, but Malcolm waved him silent. As soon as she was seated, Jane felt the excitement that horses always gave her. She signalled the horse with a gentle pressure of one leg and he took off into a smooth, controlled canter.

Jane forgot Malcolm, forgot the unacknowledged sexual impulse that had just passed between them. She felt only the delight of the motion, of the speed, of the rhythm of the horse's gait. As they approached a corner of the field she felt Risk Taker resist, spooked as some horses are by corners. Her thigh and calf muscles were already protesting; she had not ridden for years, but she forced herself to exert every ounce of pressure to direct him into the corner, then out the paddock gate and into the pasture. They swept around the pasture, back into the paddock. She signalled him to trot, to walk, then brought him up in front of Malcolm and slid off. She was sweating, but she felt triumphant. She could feel her thigh muscles trembling, and thought for a moment that she would fall, but she recovered and they walked slowly to the gate and then headed towards the house.

"I'd never have let you do that if you'd asked," Malcolm said. "But it was beautiful. You looked like my idea of a Valkyrie, riding that beautiful horse."

Jane ran her fingers through her hair, trying to recover from the thrill she had felt.

"There's just nothing as exciting to see as a beautiful woman on horseback," Malcolm said. As they approached the house, Malcolm let the distance widen between them. "Well, why not? Why not give it a try? But just for a month. And then, if Georgia still hasn't come back, we'll feel well within our rights to replace her. I'm sure I'll be able to sell it to management there, so if you want it, Jane, it's yours."

He turned and walked quickly back towards the house and Jane hurried to catch up. She was glad he had his back to her and could not see her face.

CHAPTER 8

Driving back towards the city Jane's good spirits drained away. She thought she had started something foolish that she would not be able to sustain. It was going to cause her a great deal of trouble. She would need Malcolm's respect to succeed at Prospero. And she did not think that it was respect that had caused him to give her the chance.

Whatever was she thinking of to believe she could do Georgia's job? To pretend to Malcolm that she was even remotely qualified? The idea was so absurd she felt nauseous.

Beside her in the right-hand lane was a shiny black Bronco. A family of tired, sweaty kids cuffed one another in back, periodically turning to look at her and to stick out their tongues. The parents stared straight ahead, their faces tired and withdrawn. The kids had the windows rolled down, and from time to time they would shout out things to Jane: "Hey, hey, neat car! How much did it cost?" Or, "Hey, lady, can I have a lift in your awesome car?"

"I got it used," she shouted back, and the child

to whom she had replied, covered her ears, blushed, and ducked beneath the car window. The car behind her was blaring heavy metal rock. From time to time, on the far right, a cyclist, clad in shiny lycra, face hidden in goggles and helmet, sped by. Jane thought it ironic that on a Sunday evening one could probably cover the forty miles between cottage country and Toronto faster on a bicycle than in a sports car designed for speed.

She turned her mind to the evening of Georgia's disappearance, visualizing the party as Pat had described it. A big crowd, packed into Pat's small house, the sliding doors open to the night, the air heavy with the threat of rain. Georgia and Simon had arrived when the party was in full swing. Pat had greeted Simon, directing him to put their raincoats into the spare bedroom, the same bedroom Jane had stayed in. Then she had left them to circulate, returning to talk to other friends. Pat said she didn't remember the details, only that Georgia had seemed a little tired and Simon had explained that she was working too hard. Then Simon had come to say that he was leaving and that he was giving Ivor, who he thought had drunk too much to drive, a lift home. Georgia had left earlier, perhaps because she was tired.

Simon said she had been definitely okay to drive since she had not had much to drink; she had come straight from work and was in her own car. And when Pat had checked the house, after the last guest had gone, there were no coats left. The next day, Simon called to ask her if Georgia had

come back; that was when Pat learned that
Georgia had not arrived home after the party.

Simon had seen Georgia going out the door,
putting on her raincoat, as it had started to rain.
No one had seen her since. Both Simon and Pat
had asked others if they had seen Georgia leave
with anyone, or if anyone had followed her out.
No one remembered. And that was not at all surprising, Pat had said; it had been one of those parties, the kind where, for some reason, the guests
are uncomfortable. People who like one another
and want to have a good time begin to drink too
much and the party takes on a slightly hysterical,
embarrassed tone, as those who can't hold their
liquor begin to make fools of themselves and the
rest try not to notice. Perhaps, too, Pat had said, it
was her fault that the party had not been very nice.
She had not served much food, the supper was
late and not particularly interesting—cold cuts,
lots of fruit and raw vegetables. She had not been
in the mood to go to a great deal of trouble. The
party had been a kind of afterthought. But she
made up for it with the drink, rows of different
kinds of Scotch and rye, gin and vodka. People
were getting out of the habit of hard liquor; many
people drank only wine or mineral water now,
especially when they had the long drive back to
the city to face. And there was the weather.
Although summer had arrived, that night it was if
winter had come back for a quick nip, a strange,
cold prefiguring autumn. That, plus the threatening thunderstorm, forced people back inside the
crowded room, when the party had been planned

for out on the deck. Or maybe, Pat said, she
hadn't invited a good mix of people. Perhaps
there were too many in their forties and fifties. Not
enough younger ones to let everyone feel that they
were young and glamorous and anything-can-hap-
pen people. Perhaps they had looked around and
seen others looking as worn and battle scarred as
they felt themselves. So they drank too much and
few could remember much about the party except
that it had been cold for an early summer night,
with occasional brief showers; then a terrible thunderstorm had broken just after two o'clock that
morning, so that many of them came home to find
pools of water in their houses where they had left
windows open, and woke on the Saturday to find
flooded gardens and dripping leaves to accom-
pany the inevitable hangover.

Simon had awakened to find that Georgia was
still not home. He had called the police, called all
her friends, even called Jane, who hadn't seen
Georgia for some months. He had been calling off
and on since, asking if Pat had heard anything,
getting more and more miserable. Of course, once
people realized that there had been no car accident reported, everyone's first thought would have
been—if it had been anyone but Georgia—that
she had left the party with someone else, and then
not gone back to her husband. And perhaps, she
was living with that other someone, a man—or
even a woman—and had been, since her disappearance, not able to take the consequences. And
the amount of drinking she had done that night
lent some credence to this supposition.

But not Georgia—that was the problem. Anyone but Georgia. Because there wasn't a person who knew Georgia Arnott who believed that she would have behaved in that way. And this universal conviction, among all her friends, acquaintances and colleagues—that the most likely explanation could not be right if the person in question was Georgia—was perhaps the most signal pointer to the fact that Georgia Arnott was a most unusual, a most remarkable woman.

Jane could remember vividly the first time she met Georgia. She had been invited to lunch with a friend, and when she arrived she found her friend waiting at a table set for four. "I've invited two people I want you to meet. Someone, especially, I know you'll like," Jane had been told by her friend. Then, "Look, here she is, that's Georgia. I know you're going to love her, as I do." And Jane had looked up to see who this highly praised person might be.

They had been sitting in a dark corner of a small restaurant on a bright summer day and Georgia was just coming in through the door from the street. At first, all Jane could see was her silhouette—strikingly beautiful—backlit by the strong sunlight from outside. As she came in through the doorway, Jane saw better what it was in Georgia that had so arrested her attention. It was not only the unusual qualities of her body, the graceful slope of her neck and shoulders and her narrow waist. But it was the elegance of her walk, the supple, slightly swaying motion that was so compelling. Georgia had a kind of presence that caused Jane to hold her wineglass in mid-air, halfway to her mouth, forgetting to finish the gesture. And then, as Georgia approached them, Jane saw that Georgia was ugly. Not plain, not failing to be pretty, but extraordinarily ugly.

Georgia had sallow skin and coarse dark hair, which sprang up in unruly waves from her too high forehead. On that day it was pulled back and tied behind her head, and Jane could see that the wiry brown hair was threaded with grey. Her eyes were large and slightly protuberant, her brows thick, low and straight. Her nose was very long and her mouth, full and sensuous, with the bottom lip slightly protruding. Her chin was square and masculine. It was a face which on a man might have been almost good-looking. On a woman, it was rough, strong and totally out of place. Joined on to that swan-like neck, that gracefully swaying body, the effect was a startling and almost painful incongruity. Then the friend introduced them and Georgia smiled, her brown eyes full of light and warmth and Jane forgot that Georgia was ugly, and had never remembered it since, until this moment, recalling the shock of their first meeting.

"Let's not shake hands," Georgia had said, smiling, her voice rich, her articulation elegant. "It's a kind gesture, but I see your drink hasn't reached its destination." She kissed Jane's friend and asked after her child with such affection that Jane had thought to herself that if she could have fallen in love at first sight with a woman, she would have fallen in love with Georgia. Her smile, the expression in her eyes, the humorous quality of her

· voice, her grace, had made a profound impression.

"I meant to bring Celia, as you asked me to do," she said to Jane's friend, "but you will have to put up with just me. I tried all possible means of persuasion, but she said she had something more important to do, which, it seems, was getting her dog out of the pound, and nothing could sway her. The truth is she's in a battle with her neighbour, and getting her dog released so her neighbour won't have the satisfaction of the dog being impounded for more than a few hours means more to Celia than her dearest friends, probably more than life itself. Apparently this feud is famous all over Bayview. No doubt you'd have heard of it," she said, smiling to Jane, "if you were a friend of Celia's and had the benefit of her ringside play-by-play. Naturally, the subject of dogs is not one that her friends would normally find gripping, but Celia is such a good talker we all wait with baited breath for each new installment."

Jane said that she had read some articles in the newspaper lately on the subject of unattended dogs being snatched.

"If you haven't eaten here before"—Georgia looked at Jane questioningly, and Jane shook her head—"then I advise you to stay away from the pasta and not on any occasion whatsoever to read the desert menu." Lowering her voice she read out: "Linguine made from fresh eggs and unbleached flour in our kitchen, the sauce made with pesto, tiny gulf shrimp, sun-dried tomatoes, or, how about rich cream—"

"Enough," Jane said laughing. "I get the point, I'll have the salad. . . ."

By that time Jane had recovered from the intensity of her response to meeting Georgia. She was grateful that Georgia had picked up on this and had kept chattering until Jane was more composed. Jane relaxed and the conversation moved easily back and forth among the three women. Jane found she loved listening to Georgia talk, perhaps because she spoke light-heartedly. But there was something more: Jane felt as if a powerful, larger-than-life nineteenth-century woman, a Charlotte Brontë or George Eliot, had appeared in her world, and brought with her a completely different scent—one that Jane realized she had been wanting to breathe in, in deep draughts, like fresh air.

What a strange fancy to have on meeting someone, she had thought then. And now, remembering, she thought that, in a way, she had fallen in love with Georgia when they first met. They had become good friends and Jane had spent, during those first few months of their friendship, a great deal of time with her, trying to understand what the secret of Georgia's extraordinary power could be. And then, like all infatuations, the intensity of her feelings for Georgia had worn off and they had seen each other less and less. Perhaps she had been a bit jealous when Georgia fell in love with Simon and they married. It was the first marriage for Georgia, who had been at that time about thirty-four. There had been men in her life, but not many. Georgia was too serious for light rela-

tionships. Jane had been moved by Georgia's—
Was it purity? Was that what it was? Georgia
seemed to be motivated by curiosity and by love.
Never, it seemed to Jane, by the kind of mysteri-
ous, dark urges that drove Jane to hurt herself and
others, never by ambition, by the desire to strike
back against someone who had humiliated her.
Georgia seemed never to be torn, like Jane, by a
constant battle not to do those ignoble things that
Jane felt so often driven to do.

Jane could not understand what Georgia meant
when she told Jane that she respected her, because
Jane made rules for herself and kept them: not to
sleep with married men because Jane thought it
wrong; not to sleep with people she didn't care for
because she knew that would prove to be degrad-
ing; to deal as fairly as possible in business, to be
loyal to her friends. "But I do those things for self-
serving reasons," Jane had said. "Not because I
want to; I have to force myself to behave or I'd be
really awful." But Georgia had disagreed. "No,
you're not being fair to yourself," she had said.
"You are wrong to give me credit and yourself
none. I don't do bad things because I don't want
to, can't bear to, just as I can't stand to sit through
a violent movie. It's a kind of allergy. You don't get
any credit in heaven for not doing what you don't
want to do."

Now, remembering Georgia, Jane thought, I will
find her. No possible harm can come from looking
for her. Of that Jane was certain.

CHAPTER 9

Jane was sitting at Georgia's desk, looking out Georgia's window. Beyond the parking lot there was a stretch of grass, which looked coarse but very green, as if it had been left to go wild, unweeded, unwatered, then brought back to life by an uncaring hand. Probably that was what had happened, as Malcolm has rescued Prospero when it was close to receivership and had put back in place the cleaning services and maintenance, which had been neglected. Beyond the belt of grass Jane could see another parking lot and the wall of the cinder-block building, which was Prospero's nearest neighbour in the Markham industrial park.

It was another hot bright day. The sun shone down on the black asphalt, through the brown pollution haze, and glinted off the chrome and glass of the cars parked there. Jane, who was accustomed to working in an office tower, liked being on ground level, despite the lack of a glamorous view. She liked the fact that the window of the office slid open and she could smell the fresh air, mixed with the fumes of traffic; she could hear the noise of the cars passing by on John Street, and the occasional slam of car doors as the parking lot filled up.

She was dreading her first meeting with the Crystal development group. She had arrived at Prospero at seven o'clock, hoping to have some time with Georgia's files before she met with them and took up her new responsibilities as team manager.

As Jane logged on and browsed through Georgia's directory of files, her on-line mailbox, her work schedules, she felt the enormity of the task she had taken on. It was overwhelming. Georgia's management directory contained hundreds of electronic files with cryptic names, in hierarchies Jane didn't understand. She had been told that Georgia had great organizational skills. No doubt that was so, but how was Jane ever going to understand the systems Georgia had created to manage her project?

Simon had told Jane that Georgia kept an encrypted project diary, and he had given Jane the key, the word that decrypted the files. She found the files, noting from their names that they were organized by month, stretching back over the nine months Georgia had been managing the Crystal Project. Jane called up the file for the past month, decrypted it and began to read.

While she read, Georgia came back to her. As a whiff of perfume can awaken a memory, Georgia's words recalled to Jane the love she had felt for her when they were close, the delight she had always found in her presence.

May 1, 1988
Project meeting today didn't go off as planned.
  Ivor had another new idea and all the
  efforts of the team failed to talk him out of
  it. Finally I had to threaten to make him
  revise the specs and the documentation
  himself if he wanted to add functionality at
  this late date. He backed off, but better
  keep an eye on him in case he tries to
  code his changes and slip them in without
  my noticing. Great idea, too, as are all of
  Ivor's ideas. Was he just trying to push
  again? The famous Georgia charm leaves
  him singularly unmoved. Reminder to me:
  we are all agreed—no more than four levels of functionality and NO CHANGE TO
  THE SPECS. Constant iconic box map no
  bigger than 5 centimetres.
Of the 112 bugs reported from beta test,
  site B, the team decided only 3 need to be
  corrected in the first release, and all of
  these come again from ambiguity in the
  specs. Again. Oh where in the wide world
  is the magician who can write a spec and
  get everything there is to get? On the
  other hand, what a triumph that we are
  finding so few true bugs with 3 months still
  to go for product release.
Of the remaining 109 bugs, 43 are going to
  be dealt with in the documentation, and
  the remainder are put on the release 2
  consideration list. Report 88.5.17.

The big problem is that I don't trust Ivor. That old-world courtesy he saves just for me, that smarmy sweetness. The nicer I am to him, the nicer he is to me—never an angry word. What is he thinking behind that sweetness? Nobody is that agreeable. I think he hates women; the more he smiles, the more I need to watch out. When he smiles and pats me on the arm the hairs on the back of my neck rise. . . .

May 7

Just as I feared, Ivor coded his proposed new feature and tried to slip it by me. He gave his changes to Red to integrate and Red integrated them and they work like a charm. Great improvement in the product. They came to me like two naughty boys to say: See, we did it anyway and it works great. No, they did not amend the specs. No, they have no plans for how we could alpha test and beta test the new revised prototype in time for release. No they hadn't thought through how this will affect documentation and make it too late. Yes, they knew we decided not to do this at the meeting last Tuesday. Downcast eyes, embarrassed shuffles. I felt the steam coming out of my ears but I held it in.

Called a special meeting of all the programmers and put it to them. Catherine, Terry and Larry all went off like a bunch of firecrackers. Ivor and Red tried their hotshot hacker routines and were trounced. The

peons of the development team (Terry and
Larry) beat up on them, knowing that they
were in the right. Catherine, as senior
designer, sided with Terry and Larry. I was
able to be more in sorrow than in anger as
they agreed to bag the change and put it
forward to the fabled release 2. Of course
this means they are behind schedule with
the bug fixes they were supposed to be
working on, integrating and testing. At the
end of the meeting tempers were raw and
blood was on the floor. Took them all out
for beer and pizza and got them laughing
with jokes about some of my more famous
screw ups, but the pressure is getting to
everybody. Do these guys do this so we will
never get the product out? Is that what
they really want? That way they'll never
have to face the test of meeting their own
and their peers' expectations. Think what
this job would be like if anyone, anyone at
all, had ever truly understood the soul of a
techie whose product is about to go out
the door.

May 12
Marketing came to a review meeting and casually allowed as to how they had sold
release 2 features as being part of the
release 1 product. They had to do it—customer demand. I told them there was no
way. They said to forget meeting the sales
targets the company is depending upon for
survival. I said forget meeting the release

dates the company is counting on for survival. I suggested we all go away and both "sides" try to think up 5 possible solutions to the problem and we'd meet tomorrow. After the meeting broke up Catherine said marketing destroyed the soul and made liars and cheats out of anyone who got into that line of work; Red said that anyone who made their living by lying for the company better be kept away from him or he couldn't be responsible for what he might do; Ivor said that he, for one, understood how what they did for a living turned them into slimebags, the others should be more understanding. So I had to give them lecture 23 about how we owe our jobs to the salespeople; their eyes glazed over and it was business as usual in the software industry. However, I told them they still have to come with 5 solutions to marketing's problems by ten o'clock tomorrow.

May 19
I am coming to the unpleasant and inescapable conclusion that I can't trust Ivor. Why did he agree to stay on the team if he has no respect for me? Today . . .

The telephone buzzed. It was the group secretary. "Mr Morton would like you to come to his office right away," she said.

Jane looked at her watch. "Right away? Did you tell him I have my first team meeting in five minutes?"

"Yes, I did, and he told me to cancel it and send you up to his office. A.S.A.P., he said."

"Okay," Jane said, puzzled and alarmed. "Could you show me the way?"

The secretary led Jane down corridors, up a broad flight of stairs and into a small corner office. Although Malcolm didn't actually work at Prospero, he kept an office there and had been coming in one or two days a week during the turnaround period. He was on the phone. He waved Jane to a seat in front of the desk and she took a minute to look around. It was a bare office with a big pine-veneer desk, a telephone, a computer, and a stack of files on an empty-looking credenza. Malcolm's briefcase was open on the desk and a pile of printouts was spread out beside it.

"Yes, yes, that's all under control," Malcolm was saying. "I'd got someone in here to run the team as a temporary measure, and anyway, they'd finished the development and are just putting on the final touches, so there's no problem on that side in any case. But I wanted you to know. On time? I'll get back to you on that, but I don't see why not. . . . Yes, yes, I agree, that's the worst of it. I'll call you when things are more sorted out. In the meantime, could you round up the other directors? I'd rather they hear it from you than from the newspapers."

He hung up abruptly, and rubbed his hands over his face in a curious gesture as if he were trying to wipe something away. "I've got some bad news," he said. His voice was gentle, considerate, but his face looked frozen, his expression stiff.

"They've found Georgia."

"Found Georgia?" Jane said, understanding at once, a feeling of dread, long suppressed inside her, now communicated itself to her from Malcolm's tight face and body.

"Yes . . . found her in some bush up north somewhere, almost to Parry Sound. About a hundred kilometres north of Toronto. She's dead, Jane. She's been dead for a long time."

"Dead! Dead? Georgia?" Jane tried to understood what Malcolm was telling her. "But how?"

Malcolm's voice grew even softer, more considerate, almost as if he were talking to a child. "I'm sorry. I know she was your friend. Murdered, it looks like. Strangled."

"Oh God."

"I know you were a good friend of hers and Simon's. I thought you'd want to take the day off. I'm going over to Simon's house right now. He's going to need his friends. I thought you'd want to go, too."

"Of course."

They both stood up, not looking at one another. "We'll take my car," Malcolm said. "I'll tell you what I know on the way over. Simon called to tell me about twenty minutes ago."

She followed him down the stairs and out into the parking lot. He popped up the power locks of his Jaguar and Jane got in, smelling the leather and a faint scent of an elusive perfume that reminded her of someone, whom she couldn't remember.

"I can't take it in," Jane said. "Who would want

to kill Georgia? I never knew anyone as good."

"She was a wonderful person," Malcolm said. "We were all lucky to know her. I'm not looking forward to seeing Simon. He sounded absolutely beside himself on the phone."

"What did he say?"

Malcolm shook his head, staring in front of him at the road as they turned out of the industrial parkway and on to Highway 401. "He said he knew who did it. But he sounded as if he wasn't thinking clearly, wasn't himself."

"Knew who did it?"

"Yes, he said . . . he said, 'I know who did it, there's no question about it. I killed Georgia. That's the only thing that makes any sense. I'm responsible.'"

"What could he have meant?"

"I don't know," Malcolm said.

"He loved Georgia. I know he did."

"They were devoted to one another. At least, that's how it seemed."

"That's how it was," Jane said and they were both silent. There seemed to be nothing to say.

CHAPTER 10

Simon and Georgia had a big stone house in Rosedale. It had a lived-in weathered look, and, like many of the older mid-sized Rosedale houses, lacked anything that would have made it appear valuable to an outsider. It was a plain Tudor-style house, stone and stucco, with minimal landscaping and too little land for its size. But these Rosedale houses were considered by many the best in Toronto, and certainly their cost reflected this, eight- or ten-room houses having sold for over two million in the most recent Toronto real estate boom.

The streets had a quiet, self-contained air, very Canadian. No ostentation, no particular style, just a sense of worth and stability, peace and safety from life's greater battles. This last was an illusion, Jane knew, especially since her own apartment, in a Rosedale house, had given her the same feeling when she first saw it, but had proved to provide none of these assurances.

Simon opened the door and they all stood there for a moment, frozen, awkward. Simon looked

73

terrible. His skin was colourless, lax, sunken into
folds around his eyes. His eyes were red and puffy
and half-closed, as if, at any moment, he might fall
asleep. "Simon," Malcolm said, "Simon," then he
stepped forward and put his arms awkwardly
around Simon, patting his back as he were comforting a child.

"Oh, God, thanks for coming," Simon said,
accepting the embrace with equal awkwardness
and looking over Malcolm's shoulder, past Jane,
out of his half-opened eyes, as if he were trying to
find reality outside his own bad dreams. Malcolm
stepped aside and Jane, too, put her arms around
Simon and hugged him. The skin of Simon's
cheek felt moist and sticky, as if he had been crying, and he seemed to Jane to exude a peculiar
scent, one she had smelled when her children
were very sick, a smell of cellular life breaking
down, a smell of sadness.

The three of them walked into the living-room,
which looked smaller and more faded than Jane
remembered. It was furnished in large, squarish,
upholstered furniture. There were big deep sofas
flanked by tables gleaming with French polish.
There were several faded oriental rugs. There
were piles of magazines on the side-tables, books
crammed in bookcases, too many paintings and
prints on the walls, too much bric-à-brac on the
shelves. It was, perhaps because of this, a lovely
room, full of warmth, the love of ideas, of energy,
of life, reminding Jane suddenly and painfully of
all that she had most loved in Georgia. On a shelf
Jane could see the little figures Georgia had

brought back with so much pride from Mexico, claiming they were "as good as Olmec," the Greek bowls, the Japanese Omari teapots, the small squares of Indian silk—all mementoes of Georgia's curiosity and taste. Jane could see, too, touches of the advertising man that Simon was in some of the modern touches: a Harold Town canvas, a tall, stark halogen floor lamp, a lucite end table; but these objects were encompassed and included by the overall sensibility of the room, which seemed to express so vividly the personality of Georgia.

A woman in her late sixties, wearing a dark flowered silk dress and pearls, rose up from the sofa and Simon introduced her as his mother. She shook all their hands, looking slightly bewildered, thanked them for coming, then excused herself saying she'd like to take the opportunity to make some phone calls.

Malcolm and Jane sat down on facing sofas. "Can you talk about it, Simon?" Malcolm asked. "Can you tell us what you know, what happened?" Simon came over to the sofa where Jane was sitting, across from Malcolm, sat down and wrapped his arms around his rib-cage, as if he were hugging himself.

"I can talk about it," Simon said. "It's still hard to take it in. I guess I'm numb, I can't really believe it, except in flashes. When I do, all I can think, feel, is guilt, that somehow it has to be my fault. Why was she alone? Why did I let her leave the party alone? If I hadn't. . . . It's like . . . that it just can't be true." He was silent for a moment, his arms tightening—"As if that moment, when she left Pat

Hornby's party, is like the event horizon of a black hole and she's frozen there, forever . . . about to go out the door of Pat's house . . . and if I just say . . . wait for me, I'll walk you to your car. . . ."

"Oh, Simon," Jane said, feeling his sadness, wanting to comfort him. "That's absurd, you know that's absurd."

"Yes, probably, maybe. . . ." He took her hand for a moment, smiled at her and dropped the hand as if he did not know where it had come from.

"Is that what they think happened?" Malcolm asked. "That someone murdered her after she left the party?"

"Maybe right then," Simon said, his tone bitter, "put her body in the trunk of her car and drove her up Highway 27 and then dragged her into the bush. Some kids, hiking, found her. They'd gone off the track, into the brush, as part of the game they were playing. She was wearing her party clothes . . . and her car was driven right into the bush nearby and covered with shrubs. Either someone accosted her when she left the party or she picked up a hitch-hiker . . . but she didn't do that. Never. Georgia wasn't that stupid."

"Had she been robbed?" Jane asked.

Simon squinched up his face, closing his eyes tightly, like a child who has been told not to peek. "She was wearing a little jewellery, a gold watch, her wedding band, a pin. She had some money in her purse, and credit cards. The police found all of it—her purse, the jewellery, the money— thrown away, stuffed into a hollow tree trunk a couple hundred metres from her, from her body. I guess they search the scenes of crimes a lot more closely than most people think."

"That's odd," Jane said, "it's almost as if—"

The doorbell rang and Malcolm went to answer it. He came back, followed by Ivor and Red.

Ivor was wearing a suit. He looked stiff and uncomfortable, and as soon as he had shaken Simon's hand he unbuttoned his jacket, revealing his soft, round stomach covered in a wrinkled white shirt, which drooped gently over his belt. He greeted Jane and Malcolm politely, looking from one to the other for a moment as if trying to understand why they were there together. Then he turned to Simon.

"We just wanted to say how sorry we are," he said.

"Thanks for coming," Simon said. He sounded insincere, and Jane thought he probably knew about Georgia's troubles with Ivor. However, he was polite, gesturing to the two to sit down.

"Everybody at work wanted us to express their condolences," Ivor said. "They didn't want to bother you. And Catherine, she's kind of broken up. She's hoping to come tomorrow if it's okay, and if she can get off work," he said, turning to Jane and Malcolm, and smiling as if he were joking. But there was no humour in his eyes; his expression, as he looked at the two of them, was hostile. "It's lucky we're just about finished," he said. "Georgia was indispensable. Where else would you find someone who understood programming and logic and linguistics the way she did?"

"I'd say that no one was indispensable,"
Malcolm said, his tone polite, "but Georgia came
pretty close."

Simon's mother came in through the dining-
room, which was connected to the living-room by
an arched doorway. Jane saw that she had put out
plates of cookies and a tea urn on the polished
mahogany table. She was carrying a silver tray with
small squares of shortbread. "I've put out everything I could find, Simon. Georgia had quite a lot
put by in the freezer. It's all on the plates in the
kitchen. Should be defrosted in a half-hour or so.
These were in the cupboard; I hope they aren't
stale. It doesn't look as if you've bought much in
the way of groceries since Georgia . . ." She fal-
tered, then continued in a very matter-of-fact tone,
"since Georgia disappeared."

Simon stood up with a sudden, jerky movement,
taking the plate of shortbread from his mother
and setting it on the coffee-table between the two
sofas where his guests were sitting. "Oh, Mother,"
he said, putting his arms around her, "I know how
you loved her: oh, I'm so sorry."

"Now don't start apologizing again. I want you
to stop talking like that," she said, her voice muffled as Simon pressed her to his chest.

"Maybe we should go," Red said, under his
breath to Ivor. "Coming was the point. We're
behind schedule at work. We don't have time for
this kind of thing."

Simon walked away from his mother and
opened the sliding doors at one end of the living-
room. These gave out on to a small patio where

there were two armchairs sprinkled with winged seed pods from the chestnut tree. Simon stepped out, then turned back towards them. "Jane, come outside a minute with me, will you? There's something I want to talk to you about.'

Jane followed him on to the patio. The air was hot and still, and even though the patio was shaded, Jane felt the heat after the air-conditioned coolness of the living-room. "I'm so glad you came, Jane," Simon said. He put his arms around her and they hugged one another for a minute. Jane wanted to tell Simon how she grieved for him, how dreadfully sad she was over Georgia's death. But she didn't seem to have any words for her feelings; the feelings were too strong for her to express. So she hugged Simon back as hard as she could. They both sat down on the garden chairs.

"Jane, there's something I want to say to you." His voice was soft, hesitant. "Something . . . something wasn't right at Prospero. Georgia was worried about what was going on there. More than the usual problems of getting a new software product out the door, I mean. I'm hoping you'll stay on for a while, maybe find out something. What if it was someone there, someone she was thwarting. . . ." He tailed off, looking at her.

"Why do you say that, Simon? Did Georgia tell you anything to make you suspicious?"

"Not directly. She told me about work, she brought me home printouts of her project diaries to read, so I know what a sneak that Ivor was, and how Red was his toady and Catherine too soft to go against them most of the time. But that was nothing, Georgia could handle the usual stuff. No, it was more her manner; she was worried the last few days. She wasn't herself at the party, drinking like that. Oh, God."

"Don't distress yourself like this Simon. It doesn't help."

"Jane, you could find out what was going on there. You'll read her project diary, you'll work with the people she worked with, you'll see how they act." He hesitated, then burst out, "If one of those sons of bitches killed her. . . ."

"You're not thinking straight, Simon. Surely it's more likely that she picked up a hitch-hiker?"

"No! *You're* not thinking straight. Once you've had a chance to think it over, it will be obvious to you. Come on, Jane. It's clear—someone who knew her did this, and tried to make it look like a robbery or a mugging. They thought the police would never look in the tree trunk and find the jewellery—probably they thought the body would never be found. And God knows, the police say it could have been years.

"Someone at that party saw her leave early and took their chance. I'm sure of it, Jane. Sure of it! Ivor, Red and Catherine were there. And don't forget that Malcolm lives close by."

"What are you talking about? You're not making sense."

"Maybe someone at the party, or nearby, arranged to meet her after; maybe that's why she left early."

"She'd have told you, wouldn't she?"

Simon turned his head, looking out over his

small lawn, towards the hedge that separated his house from the neighbour's. She could see only his profile: his once handsome face now flaccid and old looking, his mouth drawn in, his eyes heavy lidded. "Maybe, but if someone asked her not to tell anyone—you knew Georgia. If it was someone's secrets involved, Georgia would have said nothing—to anyone."

Despite herself, Jane was following Simon's arguments. In fact, much the same thing had passed through her mind, as soon as she heard about Georgia's purse being hidden with the jewellery inside. Why would someone take the purse and jewellery and then hide them, unless they wanted to make Georgia's murder appear to be a robbery? But she didn't want to believe this; she didn't want to believe someone close to Georgia had wanted to kill her.

"Simon," she said gently, "the world is full of crazy people. Maybe she did pick up a hitch-hiker. . . ."

"Anything is possible," he said, "but it's unlikely. She wasn't touched—there were no signs of it. She had no food to speak of in her, only booze. She must not have eaten at the party. She was on her way home; she never got here. The alarm was still set. The cat was still out. I don't care how you slice it, Jane, Georgia was murdered by someone she knew and they tried to cover it up!"

"Maybe you just want to think that, because anything else is so random and meaningless you can't bear it."

"No! Please, Jane. Even if you don't believe me,

humour me. Do it for me. I'm begging you. See
what you can find out at Prospero. Pay attention,
okay? One of those egomaniacs killed my wife, I'm
sure of it."

"Well—"

They were interrupted by the sound of raised
voices from the living-room. It was Ivor, Red and
Malcolm—arguing. Jane got up quickly, went into
the living-room and closed the sliding doors
behind her, her distress from her conversation
with Simon now turning to anger. How could they
argue when Simon was near, when something so
serious and terrible had happened?

"We don't need her, we don't need anybody,"
Red was saying. "Ivor is the senior programmer on
this, he can solve anything that comes up.
Catherine is the designer, she can do the schedules, keep on top of the paperwork. Face it, Crystal
is Ivor, Catherine and me. We designed it, we figured out how to do it, we brought it to Prospero
and made it happen. Better not forget that!"

"Is that so?" Malcolm said, his face flushed.
"Well, Crystal is a Prospero product, and when I
last looked I was the major shareholder in
Prospero." It was obvious that Malcolm was not
used to being challenged, to being talked back to.
He was furious.

"Please," Jane said, "stop all this. It's completely
out of place. Simon has enough to bear without
you shouting in his living-room about who is to
replace Georgia. We came here to make him feel
better, not worse."

"You're right," Malcolm said.

Red, his face still twisted with anger, turned away from Jane and starting walking towards the door. Ivor glanced slyly at Malcolm, a small smile passing so quickly over his face that Jane thought she might have imagined it. Then he called out to Red that he wanted to say goodbye to Simon, and after he had done so, both left directly from the garden, without saying goodbye to Jane or Malcolm.

"Not the politest guys in the world," Malcolm said.

"Well," Jane said, "probably they're upset about Georgia."

"Oh, no doubt about that, but they're usually that rude. They know we have to put up with it— it's the price we pay for their brilliance—but it gets on my nerves. I always admired how well Georgia dealt with them. Few would have the patience, the control or the tact."

"Or the smarts."

"It will be interesting to see how you handle them."

Jane sighed. "I think I should go back to work and start handling them; it looks as if it needs doing right away. If I don't get them to support me, I'm not going to get anywhere."

She went out to the garden to find Simon, now lying stretched out on a plastic chaise longue, his eyes closed, his face finely beaded with sweat and glistening in the heat. "It's awfully hot out here," Jane said. "Please come inside, this isn't good for you."

"Are you going to do it, do what I asked?" Simon said, not opening his eyes.

"Simon. . . ."

"Please, Jane. It means everything to me. It would help so much if I could get this worry off my mind."

"Well, okay, if you insist, but . . ."

"I'll talk to you in a few days, when I'm feeling more with it, and tell you everything I know about what's going on at Prospero. But it's just vague suspicions, so you're not missing anything in the meantime. And watch your step over there, watch out for that Ivor. He's an arrogant bastard and you can't trust him an inch."

His tone was so bitter that Jane was surprised. "I'll do what I can."

"I want you to really try, Jane. Promise?"

"All right, all right, I promise."

"Thanks, Jane. You don't know how much it means to me—to find out who did this will help, I know it will."

She leaned down and brushed his cheek with her own, waited for Malcolm to say his goodbyes both to Simon and his mother; then they left, walking out to the car together in silence. I hope you feel better after that, Simon, Jane thought, because I sure as hell don't. I feel a great deal worse.

As they got into the car, Jane, looking back at the house, thought she saw Simon at the window watching her. She had an uncomfortable feeling that he wanted something from her that she didn't yet understand.

CHAPTER 11

It was twelve-thirty by the time Jane and Malcolm got back to the office. Malcolm had an appointment; he dropped Jane at the door and drove on. Jane felt tired and drained. She stood at the door of Georgia's office, looking in, wondering if some essence of Georgia, some vibrations in the ether, might still be present to help her. But now that she knew Georgia was dead the office seemed somehow more daunting.

She walked over to Georgia's bookcase, which covered one wall of the office, and ran her fingertips over the spines of the books. There were volumes on philosophy and logic, on project management and software marketing, on language and artificial intelligence and mathematics. There were books on management, psychology and finance. There were binders of notes and reports.

The rest of Georgia's office was functional and expressed little of her personality: there was a big desk covered with a phoney-looking veneer, a meeting table, a credenza with a personal computer and a computer terminal.

Georgia's telephone buzzed and Jane picked it up.

It was Pat Hornby. "Jane, have you heard?"

"Yes, I'm just sitting here in her office, trying to take it in."

"I know, I can't believe it either. I can't work today, this is just too dreadful."

"I know what you mean. I went over to Simon's house with Malcolm this morning, and on the way back he asked me to stay on until I could find them someone else to take over here. But, just looking at her office, I can't concentrate on work—I keep thinking about her."

"How about we have lunch together. We can talk about it."

Pat was looking elegant. She wore a stylish grey linen suit with a wrapped skirt that made her seem slimmer than she was, a well-cut dark red linen shirt open at the throat and heavy silver jewellery. She came towards Jane smiling, then leaned over to give her a kiss and a whiff of Diorissimo.

It was a small, bright restaurant in a mall. Sun streamed in through the windows giving the place an antic cheerfulness that Jane found grating. Around them, the other diners gestured and ate looking, to Jane, greedy and artificial. She had the irrational thought that they should be showing more respect. After all, Georgia was dead.

Pat ordered a vodka tonic and Jane a Perrier. Jane wanted a drink, but she knew it would be best to keep her wits about her. She hadn't forgotten Pat's warnings when they had last met, and she wasn't sure if underneath Pat's frankness there weren't other motives. She liked and admired Pat. But Pat's curious refusal to explain herself had made Jane wary.

They chatted for a few minutes, sharing their sadness and confusion about what had happened to Georgia, speculating about why someone would want to murder her. "Of course," Jane said, "most murders are committed by someone close to the victim."

"Not this time—I don't believe it," Pat said. "Of course, it's such a cliché to say everybody loved her. And I guess it's not true. Her best qualities probably put some people off. Sometimes someone that good makes you feel ashamed of yourself. But even so, no one would want to harm her. It was so obvious that if you had a problem with something Georgia was doing, you could talk to her and work it out. And she always understood, even when she didn't agree with you. No," she said, shaking her head, "it makes more sense to think of it as a freakish accident, that somehow she met up with a psycho."

"Well, the way it happened doesn't make that very likely," Jane said. "The murderer seems to have gone to a great deal of trouble to see that she wasn't found, and if she were found, it would be hard to identify her." Jane told Pat what she had learned from Simon. "And I guess there are some people who would have liked to see Georgia out of the way. After all, let's face it, Georgia got things done, and when you do that there are people who don't like what you do or how you do it. I was reading her project diary. It looks like she had trouble with the development team at Prospero, especially Ivor."

"Aha, Ivor. You know the story behind that, I suppose."

"No, tell me," said Jane. She was being disingenuous. Malcolm had told her a little about the history of the Crystal Project; how the original idea for the project had been brought to the founder of Prospero by a team of experts. That team had been headed by a linguist named Catherine Brooks. Catherine's group had consisted of Ivor Turlefsky, a programmer, who was an expert in artificial intelligence, and two other senior programmers, one of whom, Red Kieran, was an old friend of Ivor's. The original idea for Crystal had been visionary, and, as with many software projects, the dreamers had seriously underestimated the difficulties of their task. But Catherine and Ivor had sold the idea to Prospero and been hired. They had filled in the team and set to work, and $1.5 million and eighteen months later the project had been an unmitigated disaster. That was when Georgia had been hired. But, of course, before Prospero had brought Georgia in there had been a great deal of turmoil.

Catherine had proved to be a better talker than a doer. Ivor, with Red's connivance, had pushed her aside until she had only titular power. He had then run things until Georgia was hired. It was only to be assumed that there had been a power struggle—which Georgia won—before she gained control of the project, turned it around and completed the first working prototype of Crystal. This was now in beta testing at about fifty trial sites in the U.S. and Canada. And of course it was the positive reports coming out of the test sites that had raised Prospero's image in the market and allowed the company to convince its backers to give it the money it needed to hang on through market launch.

"I can't believe Malcolm didn't warn you about Ivor. You'd be Daniel in the lions' den!"

"Well, he did tell me that Ivor had kind of pushed Catherine Brooks aside, that he had tried the same thing with Georgia, and that he might try it with me. But I'd have to put up with it, because Ivor was crucial to the success of Crystal. Apparently there aren't that many experts in artificial intelligence who are any good, let alone those who know about natural language."

"Natural language?"

"Oh, you know, that just means that the software is going to communicate with the user in English—real language—rather than computer talk. Getting a program that can take user input in English rather than special commands is very hard to do."

"Anyway," Pat said, pulling a cigarette from the pack she had placed on the table, and lighting up, "you've got to watch Ivor. He's a controller. He's very bright and he wants to run things. He's never admitted to himself that he made a hash of Crystal and that Georgia pulled them all out when they were drowning. He thinks he had everything just about fine and she came along to take the credit."

"Or so he says," Jane said. "But naturally he'd take that view of things. A guy like that, it'd be too humiliating to think anything else."

"Right. But, Jane, I think he hated Georgia. He's one of those men who can't bear to be bettered by a woman."

"I thought you just said that nobody hated Georgia."

"Well, all right, maybe not hated. But you understand what I mean."

"How do you know about all this anyway? Did Malcolm talk to you about it?"

"Sure, we're still friends. He'd got into the habit of thinking aloud in my presence. He called it talking to me, asking for my opinion—you know what I mean—the way men ask for your opinion but what they really want is for you to agree with them? Anyway, the point is, we still talk all the time. I probably know more than anybody except Malcolm about what was going on with Crystal."

"Do you really think so? I mean, Malcolm wasn't likely to know the ins and outs of things, on a daily level, was he?"

"You'd be surprised. For one thing, Georgia was very bright. She knew that the more management knows, if they get it from you, of course, the more likely they are to be onside when you need them."

Jane thought this was a view that would be widely disputed, but if Georgia could make it work, more power to her. Jane certainly told her boss, Orloff, as little as she possibly could, since he reacted negatively to everything she told him except clear and indisputable final successes. She doubted any other technique would work with him.

"Anyway, the point I'm trying to make here is, watch out for Ivor. I'm sure he wanted Georgia's job. He tried to get it by fair means and foul, but Georgia was a match for him. I imagine you will be too, Jane."

"I sure hope so."

The first of the early drinkers were coming in, in twos and threes, to continue business over cool drinks. Jane pushed around the last of her salad on the plate. The lettuce, wilting in the pools of dressing, had grown soggy and unappetizing. Thinking about Pat's portrayal of Ivor was adding to her anxieties. "What about the others?"

"I think Red is Ivor's tool, but Malcolm didn't believe it was that simple. You can forget Catherine. She's one of those intellectuals who are all abstract ideas and incapable of accomplishing any real task. Malcolm thought she should be fired, but Georgia insisted that she wanted her to stay. Perhaps it was political, she could get Catherine's help in power struggles with Ivor. Terry and Larry, the two junior programmers, are just bright young guys out of school who work hard and are oblivious to all the manoeuvring. They're good people as long as you don't try to involve them in things they don't care for. Then you'll find them not there. Apparently during the power struggles that went on before Georgia came in, they'd just not show up at the heavy meetings. So—"

"Just a minute, Pat. I'm not going to get

involved in any power struggles. I'm just there to keep an eye on things until I find a replacement for Georgia. After all, Crystal is virtually finished, it's just a question of fixing the problems that are found in the beta test." Even as she spoke Jane knew what she was saying was not true. She was, in fact, in the middle of it. Everyone knew the last little bit of a software product could be the hardest part of all. Getting a product "out the door" was considered perhaps the most challenging part of the whole cycle.

Jane put down her fork. "I really should get back to work. But before I go I've got to ask you why, when I was at your place last weekend, you told me not to try to find Georgia."

"Oh God."

"Pat, come on."

"I thought you could get hurt looking into Georgia's life, her personal situation."

"I don't understand," Jane said, exasperated. "What do you mean? What you're saying doesn't make any sense at all."

"Look—do your job at Crystal. That's going to be hard enough. Georgia's life is going to have resonances for you that could be hurtful. I'm not going to talk about it. Just drop it, okay?"

Jane felt herself getting angry. "Don't condescend to me, Pat. No doubt you're older and wiser, but what you're saying sounds like total bullshit to me. You can't just leave it at that. You have to explain."

"Maybe so, but I'm not going to. You'll have to trust me on this. We're friends, right? You know I care about your best interests."

Jane wondered. Pat's explanation of things at Prospero had, in Jane's view, thrown more light on Pat's way of thinking than it had on the people at Prospero. Pat saw human relationships in terms of power. She was a game player. She was a warm person with strong feelings, but she had been running a publishing company for ten years, manoeuvring in a rough competitive business. Did that perhaps explain her attitudes? Or was there more? Was Pat herself involved in some way and protecting herself? After all, Pat still seemed to have strong links to Malcolm. She was a friend of Simon and Georgia's. It was at her house that Georgia had last been seen alive. Could her life and Georgia's have been entangled in some way? Was Pat truly concerned about Jane, or was she protecting herself?

Pat ran her hand through her hair, then pressed it against her forehead; she pressed so hard that when she removed her hand there were white marks on her tanned skin. "Jane!" Her voice was low, urgent.

Jane looked at her, looked into those dark eyes, saw the intelligence in them and saw more—saw true concern in Pat's face.

"Please, Jane. I'll tell you everything, everything there is to know about Georgia. I've known her since we were children. I'll help you, but don't go around asking questions about Georgia, about her life. Stick with your work at Crystal and don't let Simon push you into anything. You've had a rough time these past few years. You've lost your marriage, your kids, been alone, battered around—you know what I mean. Now you have a loving relationship, a good job and maybe, if you can keep things together, a chance at getting your kids back. That should be enough to keep you busy without looking for trouble."

Jane shook her head. "You're just not making sense," she said.

Pat sighed. "Sometimes I wonder what's the good of being older and wiser if you can't save anyone from making the same mistakes you made. You are going to be very, very sorry, Jane." She fished money out of her purse, put it on the table, got up and kissed Jane goodbye.

Jane watched her go, trying to understand what Pat had said. What was Pat afraid of? Did she truly fear for Jane, or was it herself she was thinking of? And, in any case, how could Jane let such vague warnings or threats deter her from keeping her word to Simon? She remembered his face, as he turned it up to the sun—so sad, so lost. How could she let down someone she liked so much, who had suffered as he had? It couldn't be done, even if she wanted to.

The truth was, Jane thought, Pat's warnings had piqued her curiosity. Now she was more determined than ever to get to the bottom of what had happened to Georgia. Pat must be wrong. Her warnings were absurd; she hadn't given a single concrete fact to back them up. Jane told herself she had nothing to fear. She paid the bill and walked out into the street.

Coming out of the coolness, the hot air struck

her like a blow, making her feel suddenly weak. She quickened her step, ignoring it. She had a great deal to do. And she intended to do it— nobody was going to stop her.

CHAPTER 12

Jane woke up the next morning feeling extremely ill-tempered. Perhaps it was because the previous day had been pretty well all downhill.

Upon her return from the late lunch with Pat, there were two officers of the Ontario Provincial Police waiting for her. They had required her to copy all of Georgia's electronic files on to floppy disks. She had also arranged to send the files through the network to the company's mini-computer and print them out. Jane had hoped that by being courteous she might get some information about what the police thought had happened to Georgia, but they had told her nothing.

Then she had driven downtown to her office at Orloff Associates and spent the rest of the afternoon and late into the evening going over her files looking for replacements for Georgia and phoning potential candidates. She had been extremely upset to discover that many of the people she phoned remembered the last time Jane had been involved in a murder. Two years previously Jane had been hired to find a replacement for a vice president of finance who, as it turned out, had been murdered by one of his management team. Jane did not enjoy the sour jokes about her deadly job placements, nor the view, widely expressed, that anyone who tried to fill Georgia Arnott's shoes was going to suffer in the comparison, so that the job was not particularly desirable.

Now, waking, it all came back to her. Today she would have to go to the office at Prospero and call a meeting with the project team. Very soon she would have to find a replacement for Georgia or she would be held responsible for what would, under her direction, most likely be a spectacular failure of one of the most promising software launches of 1990. And the most upsetting thing of all, she had foolishly promised Simon that she would look into Georgia's death and she knew she would do so, despite her other problems and Pat Hornby's warnings.

Jane rolled over in bed and put her head under the pillow. This had the salutary effect of muffling the roar and rattle of the air-conditioner, and for a few moments she dreamed that she would just stay in bed, unplug the phone, read the big new biography of Henry VIII Tom had given her, listen to Bach and get slowly and gently plastered. The telephone cut into her reverie. It was Tom.

"Good morning, Tom," she said, trying to keep her ill temper out of her voice. After all, it was not his fault she felt so cranky. "What time is it? My alarm hasn't even gone off. What? I can't hear you, hold on a minute." She got out of bed and turned off the air-conditioner. Now she could hear, for the first time, the rush of heavy rain and the distant crackle of thunder. She realized that it had been a peal of thunder that had awakened her. She opened the curtains and looked out. The chestnut tree outside her window sagged, its leaves borne down in the rushing water and heavy, dark luminous clouds covered the sky. She picked up the phone. "I just looked out. What an awful day, but maybe the rain will cool things down."

"I'm sorry to call so early," Tom said, "but I tried you a couple of times last night and you weren't home. . . ."

His voice trailed off, and Jane, recognizing the tense tone, felt her sour temper turn to rage. He was going to go into one of his jealous fits again, and she just couldn't handle it this morning. Not on top of everything else. It was so unbearable. Why should he have these attacks of jealousy? Surely he hadn't been like this through their long, chaste courtship? She'd have noticed. Then, he had seemed so sensitive, so tender, so understanding. His patience and understanding had been part of the reason she had fallen in love. These loving qualities had soothed all the hurt parts in her. What had she done to cause him to change like this? He was so unreasonable. But of course, she told herself, I know he can't help it. Keeping her voice calm she said, "I worked late last night. I told you I was going to, remember, when you called and we talked about Georgia?"

"I called you several times at Prospero; there was no answer."

Jane got up, holding the phone between her

shoulder and her ear, and began making the bed. She knew the conversation was going to take a while. "I was working at Orloff's, Tom. I have to find someone to replace Georgia, remember? I phoned you at home about ten-thirty to see if you wanted me to stop by, but I got no answer. But you'll notice I didn't call you at six-thirty to ask for an explanation."

"I was out of milk," he said. "I tried to get you a couple of times, then I went around to a Mac's to pick up some milk and coffee."

Who cares? Jane thought. Why shouldn't you go out if you want, and why do I need you to explain it? Why do I have to account for my every minute to you? What's the matter with you, Tom? What the hell is the matter with you! But she didn't say any of this. She had asked him these questions before; they only ended with his apologizing, explaining he couldn't help himself, and with her feeling humiliated for him and hating the whole conversation, just wanting the problem to go away so they could be friends, be lovers, be kind to one another.

"I heard you and Malcolm went over to Simon's yesterday. How is he?" Tom said.

So that's it, Jane thought. Now he's jealous of Malcolm. She tried to see Malcolm through Tom's eyes. Did Tom think Malcolm was a threat because he was rich and powerful? If so, it wasn't very complimentary to Jane. She finished making the bed and began hanging up yesterday's clothes. "Simon is pretty distraught," Jane said, deciding not to pursue what she thought was the unstated accusation.

"Have you been to see him? I think you should go, if you haven't."

Tom agreed, then tried to turn the conversation back to Malcolm. Holding on to her temper with great effort, Jane refused to engage. She told Tom that she had a great deal to do and ended the conversation with an affectionate goodbye that did not express her feelings. After she hung up she threw her pillow across the room, then grabbed it and pummelled it. "So that's what you call love, eh Tom?" she told the pillow. "Suspicion, jealousy without cause. Me and Malcolm. Give me a break. Why do you have to act like such a creep?" But as she showered, fixed herself a pot of tea, and swallowed down a stale muffin, she wondered if Tom had picked up on something she wasn't facing. After all there was that business at Malcolm's farm. But, for heaven's sake, that was only a look! She had done nothing. What standard of perfection was required of her? That she wear blinkers in the presence of all attractive men? Poor Tom. What was his problem? She reminded herself that Tom's wife had left him for another man. Perhaps he was overly suspicious for that reason. Then she asked herself, for the first time, if this story about his wife was true. And even if it were, was it possible that Tom had driven her to it with the same kind of jealousy? Which came first, the infidelity or the cankerous suspicion? These ruminations increased Jane's ill temper. I will have to talk to him about this, she told herself, but not now, while so much else I have to do is so hard. I have to find a way to comfort him, learn what I can do to make him know how much I love him. This jealousy must be worse for him than it is for me. But we can't go on like this. And there's no way I could live with him, or marry him, as long as he doesn't trust me.

When Jane got to Prospero, she found Ivor and Catherine waiting in her office. They wanted the news about Georgia, they wanted to know what the OPP officers had said, they wanted to know who would be running the project. "Hey, give me a chance to sit down," Jane said. "I'm hardly in the door, it's only eight o'clock. I need a few minutes to sort of put my thoughts in order, and then I was planning to talk to the whole Crystal group together. Don't you think that would be the best way for us to get started?"

Ivor was sitting at the table leaning back in his chair looking relaxed, comfortable and friendly, while Catherine seemed tense. She looked strained to Jane: her skin, without make-up, was pale and grainy and her large grey eyes had dark shadows under them. She watched, first Ivor as he asked Jane the questions, nodding in agreement as he spoke, then Jane as she responded. When Jane or Ivor smiled, Catherine did not smile in response, just watched them as if she were trying to read something more subtle or profound or possibly something threatening to her, hidden in their words.

"Sure, of course you have to meet with the whole team," Ivor said, "as soon as possible. But let's not forget Catherine is founder of this project and I'm the former acting head. We think it would be a good idea if you had a briefing from us first."

"I could sure use one," Jane admitted. "This project is more advanced than anything I've ever been involved with. It's probably going to take me a while to get read in and, of course, I'm going to need everybody's help to get up to speed so I can be of use to you."

They both smiled, and Jane could tell that they believed her and liked her asking for their help. But she was only speaking the simple truth and they would know it whether she admitted to it or not. She was in a vulnerable position. Without Ivor, Catherine and Red's support, she wouldn't have a hope of doing her job at Prospero. Unfortunately, it would be some time before she knew if their advice was actually helpful or if it disguised booby traps.

"Do me a favour and describe Crystal to me," Jane said. "Malcolm briefed me, but I want to know what you guys think is most important about it."

"Nothing I'd like better," said Ivor, his face lighting up. "It's my favourite subject. I could go on for hours—but, hey, don't worry, I won't. Here's the quick-and-dirty version."

He walked over to the whiteboard and pulled the top off a red marker. "You know that personal computers are everywhere. But did you know that fifty to sixty percent of them are sitting on desktops, or in cupboards, unused?"

"I didn't know it was that many."

"Well, we think it is. And we—and lots of others—think that's because it takes too much effort to learn to use them if you only need them occasionally to run a spreadsheet to balance your bank account, or write a letter.

"At the same time there's more and more powerful application programs out there doing amazing things, and they all take learning. And to add to the confusion, there's three operating systems battling it out in the market-place, and each one of them has to be learned if the beleaguered end user is going to get comfortable with his machine."

He had drawn three circles on the board, labelling one "MS-DOS," one "UNIX" and one "OS/2." "And who can remember all the commands you need to use one of the computers, if, say, you're not really into it? File structure, back-up, etcetera?"

He had drawn circles for various application programs, labelling them "spreadsheet," "word processor," "desktop publishing." "So the idea behind Crystal is that it takes all these facets"—he drew a faceted circle around all the other circles—"and with a natural language interface makes them invisible to the user, crystal clear."

"Wait a minute," Jane said. "You lost me somewhere along there. What exactly does Crystal do?"

"Crystal," said Catherine, pride in her voice, "lets you talk to your computer, as you would to a human being. You don't have to know how to format a disk, or make a file, or recall a document, or load your word processor. All the stuff that you need to know the operating system to do, you can get at through Crystal instead. It puts a layer between the user and all that. So look. . . ."

She stood up, walked over to Jane's terminal, turned it on and typed in: Let me see a list of Jane's files.

Up on the screen came: Do you mean Jane Tregar?

"Wow," said Jane.

Yes, typed Catherine. But now I've changed my mind. Let me see what she wrote yesterday?

I'm not sure you are authorized, the computer typed back. Please key in your password.

"Hey," Jane said, "let me try." She leaned over Catherine and typed her password. Then she typed: Why is it raining today?

Both Catherine and Ivor smiled. "See," Ivor said to Catherine. "She's done it, too. You know, Jane, the first thing everyone does who sees this is try to blow it up. But remember, this is just a front end to an operating system."

The computer had responded: I don't understand your query. Do you want:

> Today's date?
> Your to-do list for today?
> The file called "arraignment"?

If none of the above, please rephrase your question or try my on-line help.

"It did pretty well, didn't it," Catherine said proudly. "Now try something fair, something you'd normally do on a computer you work with."

Jane typed in: Let me see a list of who has accessed Georgia's files in the last 3 weeks.

The computer screen displayed: The following people have accessed Georgia's files:

> Simon Arnott 89–5–15
> Ivor Turlefsky 89–5–16
> Catherine Brooks 89–5–17
> Red Kieran 89–5–17
> Jane Tregar 89–6–23

For a short-form request next time type: wholsdate

"Wonderful," Jane said. "But what were all you people doing in Georgia's files?"

"I've been running things since Georgia disappeared," Ivor said. "I needed her records. Probably Red and Catherine were looking for project information too. Georgia kept things so well organized."

"Did you go into her files when she was here?" Jane asked.

Ivor looked a little embarrassed. "Hey, I just looked at what I needed to get the job done."

"I'm not criticizing, just curious," Jane said. "We've got to work together now. I've been put in charge, but you know the project and I don't. Without your help I'm not going to be able to accomplish anything. Will you help me?"

"Of course we will," Catherine said. She smiled at Jane, her sad eyes untouched by the smile, her voice sincere and generous.

"You can count on us, Jane," Ivor said. "This project means everything to our team. We've invested three years and all our best ideas in it. We want to see it succeed more than anything else in the world."

"Yes," said Catherine, looking past Jane, her eyes seeming to express some kind of profound disappointment, "we'll do everything we can. You can count on us."

"That's good," Jane said. "I'm going to need all the help I can get."

CHAPTER 13

"What the hell is it?" Orloff said. He was leaning back in his desk chair, looking out his window. Outside, strings of lumpy black clouds were passing under a bank of heavy grey overcast. Periodically a spit of rain struck the windows, reminding Jane of a snare drum announcing the arrival of an important person. There was no doubt that she was not the important person, at least not to Orloff. He was treating her in the way he usually did—with a mixture of barely suppressed irritation, heavy irony and disdain.

Jane looked out the window too. Beyond Orloff she saw rows of lit office windows. She wondered how many other people were, at this very minute, confronting unpleasant, intimidating bosses.

"It's a kind of front end to the popular operating systems that uses natural language and artificial intelligence," she said. "The idea is that it makes it a lot easier for the inexperienced person to use a computer or to use a new application. Prospero demonstrated it at the major trade fairs this year, Comdex and Hanover, and it was the hit of the shows. The trade press think it's going to be the biggest software product the industry's seen since the introduction of Lotus 1-2-3."

"I don't know what you're talking about," Orloff said irritably. "As far as I am concerned, computer applications are all Greek—except that I know Greek." Jane knew Orloff was just trying to annoy her. Computer companies were big business. And due mostly to her, many of the largest firms in the business were Orloff customers, and where his business was concerned Orloff was always *au courant.* If a product affected a company's balance sheet, or was written up in the business press, Orloff would be up on it. Orloff knew what she was talking about.

"And, anyway," he said, "I thought all that artificial intelligence stuff was hogwash. Didn't you tell me that yourself?"

"Not exactly. I said a lot of people think it's hogwash."

"It seems to me you said people with money to invest think it's hogwash. Which is more to the point. If Morton has a lot of money invested in vaporware, that's something I'd like to know about. So don't try to sell me with hype if the thing isn't real."

It was just like Orloff, Jane thought, to first profess ignorance of one of the biggest successes in the software-application industry and then to toss in an in-phrase like "vaporware," a term that referred to products that were promised and promoted, but never materialized. And though she wanted to defend Crystal, because she was already beginning to feel proprietary and to care about it, and because she knew that Orloff traded gossip the way some people trade stocks and bonds, she tried to be fair. "I guess some people believe that Crystal is vaporware. But if it works as it's supposed to, it could revolutionize the way the average person uses computers."

"So finally, Tregar, we get to the nub." He slid open a desk drawer and took out a small bottle of ink and a thick piece of his cream-coloured monogrammed personal stationery. "Is Crystal going to fly? Is Morton going to be able to pull it off without Georgia? Are they going to launch in October?"

"I'd say so," Jane said, her voice, despite her best intentions, tentative. She leaned back in her chair, the leather seat creaking noisily as she shifted her weight.

"You'd say so, you'd say so. Of course you would. That's your job right now. And I guess, the way you've manoeuvred things, it's partly up to you. But give me your worst case scenario."

"Worst case?" She watched fascinated, as Orloff took the small rubber top off the ink bottle and began to fill his Mont Blanc pen, shaking drops off on to the sheet of vellum. The small black ink drops spread into the soft paper, creating a blotchy pattern. "Worst case is that Prospero can't get the last few bugs out, or doesn't find them, or there's some fundamental flaw in the thing, or they don't finish in time for launch, or that Crystal doesn't live up to expectations. But I don't think any of that is likely. I've seen it; I think it's amazing."

"Competition?"

"That's the whole point. Nobody's been able to do this yet. They should have at least a year's lead."

Orloff laid his pen on the paper and replaced the cap on the ink bottle and the bottle in the drawer. Another small drop of ink formed on the paper, spreading ominously. "What about someone stealing the technology behind this great breakthrough? Wouldn't that put a crimp in things?"

"Stealing?" Jane said. She was shocked, partly at the idea, partly that she'd never considered it herself. Could that have anything to do with Georgia's disappearance? Obviously, however, Orloff had given the matter some thought.

"Did it ever occur to you, little Miss Tregar, that that's what happened to Georgia Arnott? That she ran afoul of some rather nasty industrial espionage."

"That's impossible!" Jane said. "Even if you got into the system and looked at the work—that wouldn't be enough. First of all, very few people could understand it. And then, configuring the product, bringing it to the market—no, no, stealing it wouldn't be worth it. Anybody smart enough to understand what was stolen would insist on writing it himself. No, that only happens in the movies and on TV."

"Nice to see you so confident. Although I can't imagine why. But how about this scenario? From what you say, if this thing takes off, it's going to be worth big money, right?"

Jane nodded.

"So say somebody convinced Georgia to sell them the secrets and to help them make a product out of it. Then when they basically had the technology in the bag, they offed Georgia."

Despite her best intentions, Jane was getting really angry. "Everything else you've been proposing is maybe possible, though I'd think pretty unlikely. But Georgia selling secrets is impossible. Absolutely."

"Nice to know you can look inside of someone and know everything about them, Ms Tregar. You're obviously in the right profession. Care to give a seminar on this to your elders and betters? None of us are that infallible."

"Oh, it's not that at all, Eddie. You know that's not what I mean. Do you know anything about Georgia, anything about her background?"

"Tell me." He smiled, reached into his drawer again, pulled out a Kleenex and began carefully wiping the pen, polishing it.

"It's a long story, but the short version is this. Georgia's father was a very rich man. He died when Georgia was a little girl, and her mother remarried and had another daughter. Georgia's mother inherited all the money, and Georgia lived with her stepsister. The stepsister was very beautiful and Georgia—Did you ever meet her? No?— well, to put it nicely, Georgia was not beautiful. Anyway, Georgia's mother was quite a famous beauty, and she favoured the sister. You'd think that would make Georgia jealous, but it didn't. Then Georgia's mother died. She left all the money to the sister. That happened when Georgia

was just starting graduate school. It turned out that
the stepsister's father was the trustee and he kept
control of the money so that Georgia couldn't get
any at all. And don't forget, it was her own father's
money. But they wouldn't give her any. Everyone
told her to fight it, that she'd win, that it was clear
that her father never meant this to happen. And,
in any case, there was a couple million; enough for
all three of them. But Georgia wouldn't fight. She
said she loved her sister and wouldn't do anything
to hurt her. Georgia worked her way through graduate school, which wasn't easy because there
weren't a lot of part-time jobs for students then.
She lived in really miserable conditions, but
Georgia never said a word against her sister. She
always spoke of her with love and compassion. The
fact is Georgia wasn't motivated by money. It
didn't interest her. She never talked about clothes,
or cars, or jewellery or her salary, or anything like
that. Ask anyone who knew her. Georgia was always
loyal. Georgia sell out Crystal? Pigs will fly first!"

"Tregar," said Orloff, balling up the ink-stained
piece of paper and tossing it into his waste-basket,
"you're painting a picture of a saint here, and—
take it from me—there is no such animal, in this
day and age anyway. She's too good to be true.
Also, she sounds loathsome."

Jane stood up. "I have quite a lot on my plate
right now," she said. "I'm still looking for a replacement, plus I'm caretaking the Crystal team. Do
you need any more information? If not . . ."

"Calm down, calm down. I didn't mean to insult
your idol. No doubt Georgia Arnott was the

Second Coming, if you say so. The fact that she was murdered is, of course, a pure fluke."

Jane sat down. On that point, she thought, Orloff was right. She knew it; he knew it. Either Georgia had been killed as part of a mugging, which Jane didn't believe, or her murder grew out of the person she was. And being a "saint" didn't seem to fit with that.

"I know what you mean," she said. "I guess I don't know what to think. Could everyone who knew her and loved her be wrong?"

Orloff smiled his wolfish smile at Jane. "I guess that's your problem, Jane. Because if Georgia was killed over some kind of shenanigan over Crystal, you should be watching your back. And if she was killed because she wasn't the lily-white angel you think she was, I think you're going to be pretty devastated. I don't know why, but it looks to me as if you've got too much invested in the goodness of Georgia Arnott. I'd strongly recommend that you grow up or you are going to take a real tumble over this one. And you know where I stand on that."

"You don't give a damn," Jane said bitterly.

"Did I say that? Not at all. At Orloff Associates we only want success and happiness for all our associates, no matter how they get themselves promoted to associate." His voice was serene, and this time only the small tremor at the corner of his mouth, perhaps a smile, perhaps a grimace of dislike, revealed the pleasure he was taking in what he regarded as Jane's inevitable downfall.

CHAPTER 14

At Prospero, people were being helpful, politely pointing out things she had not thought of, deferring to one another, being tactful. No doubt it was her "honeymoon"; probably they were pulling together now because Georgia was dead, because Malcolm had insisted that there would be no Crystal if the team did not support Jane, and because they all had so much invested in Crystal. Or were they pulling together because they were frightened? Frightened of what she might find out if there were a rift in the team, in their solidarity, that allowed her to discover more than they wanted her to know?

Certainly the level of tension in the whole company was extraordinarily high. And the Crystal group was in an even worse state, suffering the inevitable stresses of the period directly before a new product launch. Jane knew that the politeness was only a veneer, but she was not sure what it was covering up.

Once Orloff had put the idea of industrial espionage in her head, she found herself suspicious of actions she was sure she would have trusted under ordinary circumstances—if there were any ordinary circumstances in the software business—something she often doubted.

The day after her meeting with Orloff she decided to come in early. As launch approached, the team was working longer and longer hours and it was not unusual to find the programmers there most of the night. Sometimes she stayed with them, sharing the midnight pizza and being there as a sounding board when they needed her. Other times she came in very early, say six-thirty, to lend encouragement.

But today she didn't think any of them would be in early, as they had just completed a long push and she had told them to take it easy. She had said she, too, would be sleeping in, but waking early that morning, feeling restless and anxious, she changed her mind.

When she drove in at six she was surprised to see the light on in her office. In the parking lot she saw Ivor's dirty green BMW parked in the first slot, the one that, by unspoken courtesy, was usually left for Malcolm. As she walked down the corridor towards her office, she wondered if it were Ivor who had turned on the light, if it might be Ivor himself who was in her office. And if it were Ivor, what was he up to? Anything he wanted to know he could probably find in her computer files and he could easily access those from his own terminal.

As she approached her office, the rectangle of light shining out of its open door vanished. In the

dimness of the hall she saw a figure leave her
office and walk down the corridor away from her.
It was Ivor and he was carrying a sheaf of files. She
stood still, staring at him until he turned the corner and was out of sight. Then she went into her
office, shut the door, hung her suit jacket on the
hook and sat down at her desk.

Jane normally cleared her desk before leaving
work. It was exactly as she had left it, pristine,
except for the in-out baskets loaded with files, and
a sheet of paper with her crucial actions items for
the day, centred on the desk, just where she had
placed it before leaving.

She rifled through the files stacked in her in-out
baskets. There was nothing of interest there now;
she didn't believe there had been the morning
before, when she was last in either.

What could Ivor have taken? She thought of
looking through the files in Georgia's filing cabi-
net, but that seemed pointless. Although she had
skimmed through them from time to time, she
didn't think she knew them well enough to notice
if anything was missing. She ran her fingers
through her hair and rubbed her scalp. Then she
opened up the desk file drawer. It was empty—all
the files had been removed.

But why? These were her personal files. What
could interest Ivor in them? After all, most of her
files were at Orloff. Only things she might need on
a daily basis were filed in that drawer. She tried to
recall what she kept there. There was the file about
her child-custody case: letters from her lawyer,

copies of hers to him, court documents. Surely Ivor wouldn't care about that.

What else was there? A few letters from friends, a note or two from Tom, who sometimes wrote her at the office when he was out of town. Oh . . . and her files from the search for Georgia's replacement. She kept a duplicate set at Prospero. Résumés of potential candidates for Georgia's job, other information about the candidates, notes about ongoing negotiations—the last thing she would want Ivor to see.

This was bad, she thought, but it was not that bad. Ivor might want to compete for the position; he might think having inside information would help him. But the fact was that Malcolm would never allow Ivor to become a senior manager.

Then, she had a sudden sinking feeling. The Crystal marketing plan had been in that drawer. It was marked Company Confidential and was supposed to be kept locked up, but Prospero was pretty relaxed about things like that and Jane hadn't taken it seriously. But that was before, before Orloff's suggestions had opened her mind to the possibility of industrial espionage.

In the marketing file were the sales strategies for Crystal: the advance orders, the projections, the special arrangements worked out with wholesalers, dealers, distributors and OEM's. The main selling points that had emerged from the long tests at customer sites. This would be invaluable information for any potential competitor. What was Ivor up to? Had he just been snooping around and taken what he could find, or had he been looking for the marketing file? Jane remembered that she had had it on her desk the morning before and had been studying it when Ivor had come in to talk to her. Most likely Ivor was someone who could read papers upside-down; he'd picked up on what it was and come back for it.

Of course, there could be an innocent explanation, she thought, or relatively innocent. Ivor saw himself in constant battle with marketing over decisions relating to Crystal's launch. The file would be useful to him in that struggle; his taking it didn't have to suggest that he was involved with a competitor. Still, it didn't look good. One thing was certain: she didn't want Ivor to know that she knew. No doubt he intended to copy the files and return them.

Quickly she got up from the desk, leaving the drawer unlocked. She put on her jacket, turned off the light and left the building as silently as she could. But when she started up her Triumph, the engine turned over with its usual noisy roar. She looked up at Ivor's office window, and thought she saw, for an instant, his face looking down at her car. But it was hard to be sure because the early morning sun, low in the sky, was reflecting off his window and shining into her eyes.

When Jane came into the office again at 8:30 A.M. she found all her files replaced. She only hoped that Ivor had not seen her, had not seen her car leaving the lot. It was hard to avoid the thought that if Ivor were involved in industrial espionage, and if this industrial espionage were

connected with Georgia's death, Jane herself
might now be in real danger. If Jane were not so
angry—angry at herself for leaving the file in the
drawer, angry at Ivor for deceit—she would have
been frightened.

By noon Jane was feeling better. She was a great
believer in using work to quiet anxiety, and in that
respect it had been a good morning. She had gotten through a big stack of crucial management
paperwork. Ivor had signed out for the day, so she
could postpone confronting him for a while at
least. She had managed to persuade two promising replacement candidates to consider Georgia's
job and had set up preliminary interviews.

She had called a meeting with the marketing
group and asked them to tell her what were
Prospero's risks from potential competing products. They had assured her that if Crystal were
released on time, no one could compete with the
launch. It was too late. The marketing was too
advanced for anyone to catch up this season. In a
few months, perhaps, once Crystal was out and
had established its market—but who would be able
to match the technology? They were too far ahead.

Suppose someone could match it, she had said.
Let's pretend that someone has access to our technology and knows all our marketing plans, would
we be in trouble? But neither the marketing people nor the director of sales were particularly worried about this possibility.

Just get it out on time, they'd told her. Then no
one can touch us. Even if the whole technical
group went into competition with us and worked

night and day, they couldn't get a new product out, set up marketing channels and get to market in less than six to nine months. And even if they did pull that off, we'd be okay, because just as they got their competing product out, we'd be coming out with release two of Crystal, which will be tested, integrated and ready to go by then. Georgia thought all this through, they told her, we're protected. A person with no experience in the software business, no experience in marketing, might believe that they could compete, but they'd lose their shirts. Don't worry.

And Jane realized with some relief that Georgia had been ahead of her. If Ivor, Red and Catherine had come to Prospero as a group, they could leave as a group. Georgia had foreseen the possibility and communicated it to the marketing people. They were prepared. Of course, Ivor wouldn't know this. If he had seen her this morning, realized she knew he took the files—if she had an enemy in Ivor—well, she herself might be in serious trouble but at least Crystal itself was not at risk.

The phone buzzed and the secretary put Pat Hornby through. "Hi, Jane, how're you doing?"

Jane smiled, happy to hear Pat's cheerful voice. "Fine," she said, not wanting to burden Pat with her worries. "How are you?"

"Overworked and underpaid. Listen, feel like going shopping with me after work today? I've got a black-tie thing coming up and I've grown out of everything I own. I could use a friend when I face those three-way mirrors."

"I'd love to," Jane said. "And I'll take you for a

drink after, to help you recover."

"Thanks, Jane. I appreciate it. Can you meet me here at, say, seven?"

Jane sat on a small chair in a large dressing-room at Creeds watching Pat struggle to zip up a grey chiffon dinner dress. All the dresses Pat had tried on had been, Jane thought, absolutely lovely. "It's gorgeous," Jane said. "I'd give my eye-teeth to be able to afford something like that."

"I'd give my eye-teeth to be able to fit into it," Pat said, grunting as she sucked in her stomach and tugged at the zipper. "But didn't you divorce a rich husband? And Orloff pays well. Seems to me you wouldn't have any money problems."

"I don't really," Jane said. "It's all relative. I have enough money as long as I don't try to live rich, which I can't afford."

Pat laughed. "But your husband?"

"I didn't take anything from my husband," Jane said.

"Why not?"

"I didn't want anything of his—except the children. And I didn't get them."

"Okay, I can tell from your voice you don't want to talk about that, and I don't blame you. Ex-husbands aren't my favourite topic either. But life's ironic, eh? You've got the body for the clothes and I've got the money." She unzipped the grey dress, shimmied out of it, sighed and pulled a black silk tent-shaped dress, low-cut with spaghetti straps, down over her head. "I guess I should just expose the boobs and cover the rest, right? Best to leave it to the imagination. If I don't go to a spa or something pretty soon, I'll be too fat to shop at Creeds. I don't think their clothes go beyond a size sixteen, and there's not many of those."

"I think you're beautiful the way you are," Jane said truthfully.

"Thank you, I needed that. Anyway, how do you stay thin?"

"Oh, I'm not thin," Jane said. She, too, struggled with excess weight, which, she thought, had the tendency to make her small frame look like a dumpling. "But when I worry, I stop eating, so right now I don't have a problem with it."

"What's worrying you?" Pat turned around slowly, examining herself carefully in the three-way mirror. The dress set off her tanned shoulders, arms and breasts, but then hung like a dark shroud to mid-calf.

Jane opened her mouth to reply, but a saleswoman bustled in with more dresses, fussed over Pat, tried some belts and sashes, then bustled out again. "Oh, product launches are always hard," Jane said. "And of course I can't help grieving over Georgia, worrying about what happened to her, what it means. And thinking about poor Simon, and how I'm letting him down because I still don't have a clue about what happened to Georgia."

"Oh, Jane!" Pat said, exasperated, turning from her reflection to look down at her. "I was hoping you'd given that up."

"No, I'm sorry, Pat, but I don't intend to do that."

"God, you're stubborn. I guess you'll just have to talk to Ariela."

"Who?"

Pat shook her head. "Had they but ears to hear and eyes to see. Ariela, my sweet—Simon's first wife. You should talk to Ariela. She knows more about Georgia than anyone except Simon, and what he knows . . . well, take it from me, you have to talk to her. That's all."

"First wife?" Jane said, astounded. "I didn't know Simon was married before."

"Exactly my point. There's a hell of a lot you don't know, and you're not going to like any of it."

Jane was getting annoyed. "I'd appreciate it, Pat, if you stopped treating me like a baby. I'm thirty-five years old and, strange as it may seem, I can deal with the fact that someone has been married before."

"You're right. I'm sorry. I didn't mean to treat you like a child. It's just that . . . oh, to hell with it."

She reached over and picked up her purse, took out a pen and a pad and her date book, checked the addresses and wrote out Ariela's on the pad. "Here's her address and telephone number. She's a poet; she works mostly at home, unless she's on the road doing readings. You should talk to her. Ask her about Simon, about Georgia, about herself. See what you make of it."

"I don't understand you, Pat," Jane said. "But if you think talking to Ariela will help, I'll do it. Can I say you gave me her name?"

"Sure, but do me a favour and tell her that I told you nothing. For a while I was Ariela's confidante, big sister, whatever, you know? She's a hero-worshipping kind of person, and I attract them. She told me her secrets; she trusted me not to repeat them and I'd like her to know I haven't. Of course, we publish her, and for a poet, she's quite a good seller. You'll see why when you meet her—very promotable, quite the sex bomb. As her former friend and her current editor, I'd just as soon she knew I hadn't let her down. Okay?"

Jane nodded. She helped Pat decide on a dress, the best of a poor lot, as Pat said, and they walked out together into the street. It was still light and they strolled over to Yorkville to have a coffee at an outdoor café. As they walked they talked of other things: clothes and diets and job pressures and weather. And all the while, Jane puzzled over Pat's behaviour. Why was Pat so uneasy and secretive, so supportive and yet so unhelpful? Why did she seem so concerned and protective about Jane? As if Jane were a child who was about to find out there was no Santa Claus? It didn't make any sense.

CHAPTER 15

Jane had to go to court. It was the hearing on her request for joint custody of her children. But about two hours before she was to leave the office, she received a telephone call from her lawyer.

"I'm sorry, Jane, I have bad news for you."

She felt her stomach muscles tighten; she broke out into a sweat, felt it moisten her hands and trickle down between her breasts. Her husband had thought of something new; she was going to lose another round. How many times had he done this? Too many. No matter how much she spent on legal fees it was never enough; he spent more, bought better talent, bettered her every time.

She had known when she began this fight that he wouldn't fight fair, knew that even if she won, she risked his sending the children to Switzerland permanently where they would be beyond her reach. She had decided to fight him anyway. But before becoming entangled in the legal system, she could not have imagined the frustration, the delays, the illogicalities, the unfairness. Knowing it was her lawyer on the telephone was enough to bring on all the symptoms of a panic attack before the man had even said a word.

"Better prepare yourself for something you're not going to like—this is a rough one."

"All right, all right, I'm prepared. What is it?"

"The kids have made a motion through their own lawyer. They say they want to stay with their father exclusively."

"What?"

"They're trying to get an injunction to stop you—"

"They what?" Jane couldn't understand what the lawyer was telling her. The kids were only thirteen and fifteen. How could they have a lawyer? And why in God's name would they do such a thing? They loved her, as she loved them. She knew they did. Their love for her and hers for them was the bedrock of her life, the one thing that couldn't change, couldn't alter no matter what she said or they said. No matter if their father had kept her from them for the past three years; there had been letters, phone calls.

"They say you have shown no interest in them, never taken advantage of your visitation rights, that you—"

"Wait a minute! What are they talking about? There must be some mistake."

"Look, Jane, I know it isn't true, any of it. We'll have to fight it. I don't know yet if this is your husband speaking in the name of the children, or if someone has been putting pressure on the kids to do this."

"Bernie would never do that to the kids. It

would be too harmful to them. No matter what I think about him, I know he loves the kids. It was for the kids' sake, to get them a full-time mother, that he left me. My God, why is he doing this to me?"

"Now pull yourself together, Jane. It's not like you to panic and go to pieces like this. Just let's be rational and take this one step at a time; we just have to . . ."

Through Jane's open door she saw Ivor coming towards her. She had begun to weep and she waved him away and swivelled her chair around so that her back was to the door. "Give me a minute, I'll be okay."

Jane told herself to get control, to calm down, to think logically, but she was too upset. Her mind racing, she remembered the times over the past few years when she had tried to see the children for anything more than a brief visit. Bernie always had a reason why it wasn't convenient. And always, the reason related to the children's best interest. She had never wanted to argue, to interfere with what was best for the children. Two young boys, with their hockey tournaments, their exams, their summer camps and winter holidays, their school play rehearsals, their visits to their friends. Whatever she had to offer them was never as good, always it seemed meagre by comparison with the plans their father had arranged. Now she saw she should have insisted. But how? How to be so selfish as to say: No, they shouldn't go to Jamaica for Christmas—they should come and spend it with me in the Rosedale apartment? No, they shouldn't have a weekend in New York, to go to concerts and galleries—they should spend it helping her build bookshelves and take in a movie at the local Cineplex.

Why hadn't she just said what she felt? I love them, I want to see them, time is passing, they're growing up. They're my children too. But she hadn't felt able to say it, to insist upon taking them from a home with a loving father and loving stepmother to an apartment with a mother full of self-doubt. The kids were always polite when they phoned to postpone a visit, but now she realized that with time they had become more and more distant and she saw them less and less, so that they all felt constrained in one another's presence. She feared they had too much, were too indulged, were growing arrogant, spoiled, snobbish, but she couldn't show any of that concern in the brief time they had together. Eventually she had come to believe that they were growing contemptuous of her and of the way she lived. But it was all out of love for them that she had borne not seeing them, accepting with pain each refusal, each postponement. How could that acceptance now be held against her—be called indifference, set down in black and white in papers before the court, called neglect, called lack of love? Repetitive, half-formed thoughts, emotions, overcame her: self reproach, astonishment at what a fool she'd been, at the enormity of her mistake. She could hardly take in what the lawyer was telling her. Finally she put him off, hung up the phone, knowing that she needed time alone to think, to decide what to do, how to fight, to get back her nerve.

The telephone buzzed; it was Ariela returning her call. With an effort, Jane forced her thoughts about her children and her emotions into the place in her mind where she kept things too painful to think about, and shut the door on them. The effect was tranquillizing.

"Hello? This is Ariela. You left a message on my answering machine that you wanted to talk to me about Georgia Arnott?" The voice was soft, melodious, slightly hesitant, with a girlish overtone that grated on Jane's nerves.

"Yes, I was a friend of Georgia's. There's something I need to discuss with you. Could we get together?"

"Of course. Simon has told me all about you. I'd love to meet you."

"Good," Jane said, her own voice sounding flat and cold in her ears, in comparison to the sweetness and enthusiasm of Ariela. "Would you like to come here to my office in Markham? Or would it be more convenient if I came to your place, or if we met somewhere downtown? Or you're welcome to meet me at my apartment in Rosedale."

"Well, whatever you like, Jane. I know how busy people like you are. Why don't you come over here for tea after work? I live in the Annex, so it's not far from your place. When do you finish? Eight? Would you like some dinner then? . . . No, of course not, it's no trouble at all. I don't cook, so I'll just get some salads from the deli or

something. . . . Oh, no, I couldn't let you bring
something. Well, if you really want to . . . at eight
then."

Jane hung up and stuck out her tongue. She
tried to imagine the normally controlled, practical
Simon with someone as treacly as Ariela sounded.
A sex bomb, Pat had said. Jane wondered if Ariela
had invented her own name. It had the same
phoney sound as her voice, now that Jane thought
about it. She set the question of Ariela aside and
turned to her work. There was a lot to do before
she left the office, and with a small stab of pain she
realized that she had better make an appointment
with her lawyer for the next day. She'd have to rev
up the fight with Bernie; she'd have to go on the
attack. She could not let the children think she
didn't want them. Before, all she had had to lose
was something she didn't have—custody of the
children. Now, it seemed, the battle was for something bigger, something she didn't dare lose,
something that meant everything to her. She
pulled a pad of paper towards her, opened her
appointment calendar and began to make a list of
the times she'd tried and failed to see her children
over the past three years. It was a very long list.

CHAPTER 16

Ariela lived in an elegant old mansion on Brunswick Avenue in the Annex, one of the most charming and colourful areas in Toronto. In this neighbourhood lived immigrant families who had settled there in the forties and fifties when the neighbourhood was cheap, University of Toronto students packed into rooming-houses and rented rooms in converted mansions, and wealthy professionals lived in large renovated houses.

The narrow streets were lined with old chestnut trees. The polyglot inhabitants made strong organized efforts to get along, lobbying the city to keep out expressways, street widening and apartment buildings. It was safe to walk in the Annex at night, and on summer evenings people sat out on their converted front stoops in deck chairs, drinking beer or more upscale tipples, and greeting their neighbours who strolled back from the neighbourhood stores with groceries or flowers.

Ariela lived on the second floor of an old, unrenovated townhouse, her front bay window screened from the street by the leafy branches of a

chestnut tree. The window-ledge was full of dusty
potted plants, so that the low evening sun could
barely penetrate into the living-room. The walls
were lined with prints and paintings from floor to
ceiling, except where there were bookshelves. The
floor was covered with faded dingy Persian carpets,
overlapping one another; the furniture was rattan
with deep purple, wine-red and green flower-print
cushions, which echoed the colours of the carpets.
In all this dimness and texture, Ariela stood out.
She was a tall, slender woman with thick, wavy dark
red hair which, parted in the centre, partly covered her eyes and fell in waves halfway down her
back. She had very pale skin, a small slightly
uptilted nose sprinkled lightly with freckles, and
large luminous green eyes, the colour Jane recognized as being from tinted contact lenses. Her eyes
were dramatically made up with heavy black lines
around them, smudged slightly for effect. She was
dressed in black—a black tank top displaying small
high breasts, a wide black leather belt with large
silver studs, black jeans, tight over her small waist
and narrow hips, and black ballet slippers. She
also wore wide silver bracelets, silver rings on all
her fingers and large silver hoops in her ears. The
effect was dramatic; Jane saw immediately why Pat
had called her a sex bomb.

"I'm so glad you could come," Ariela said in her
soft, breathy voice, stretching out her arms and
drawing Jane into the living-room, her touch
caressing. She took the pizza Jane had brought
into her kitchen and came out with it on a large
brass platter. Then she went back to the kitchen,

returning with a bottle of red wine, two amber cut-glass wineglasses and an ashtray. The two women sat down on cushions on the floor, in front of the window-ledge. Ariela unrolled a length of paper towel and spread it out as plates. She poured the wine, her hair falling over her eyes. She brushed it away with a graceful, sensual gesture, tucking it behind her ears which, Jane noticed, were very small and almost pointed at the top. "What a gorgeous pizza," Ariela said. Jane grimaced, but Ariela didn't notice. Jane cut the pizza and helped herself, wiping her fingers on a piece of paper towel.

"Let's drink to Georgia . . . to having known her." Ariela said, raising her glass. "To Georgia—the best person I ever knew, or am likely to know—may the good that she did live after her, and the memory of her goodness endure."

Jane felt her distaste for Ariela vanish, as if it had never been, a rush of affection replacing it. It seemed that Ariela, too, had loved Georgia as she had. "A beautiful toast," Jane said, raising her glass. The two women smiled at one another and drank.

"How did you know Georgia?" Jane asked.

Ariela's expression grew sad. She looked down, tilting her head gracefully, so that her hair fell forward, hiding her eyes. "I guess you could say Simon left me for Georgia. But that's not exactly right." She looked up at Jane, tucking her hair behind her ears. Jane looked back, into Ariela's clear green eyes, sensing in her look a powerful, self-deceiving sincerity.

"Simon is a lot older than me, you know," Ariela said. "I met him when I went to work for his agency as a copy-writer. It was a summer job, when I was still in university; that would be about six years ago, I guess. I fell desperately in love with Simon. . . . I've always had this thing for older men . . . my first lover, when I was sixteen, was one of my high school teachers. . . . He was married and it turned into quite a mess. Anyway, Simon fell in love with me, too; I dropped out of university and we got married. But . . . I was very young, just starting to write, I met this poet and after one of his readings . . . Simon found out and he had a lot of trouble with it. Well, things weren't going very well with us. . . . Am I boring you?" she said, breaking off, and looking up from her wineglass, which she had been twisting between her fingers.

"Not at all," Jane said truthfully.

"I'm really not suited to a big house, and entertaining business friends and mothers from old Toronto families and having dinner parties and all those things. . . . So then, anyway, we met Georgia, and we both fell in love with her. She was like that, you know?"

"Yes," Jane said, "I know what you mean."

"And I could see how good she would be for Simon. So one day, when he was complaining about this and that and the other thing, my lover and the laundry and, you know . . . I just said, 'Simon, I think you should marry Georgia.' He was absolutely shocked, I don't think it had ever occurred to him."

"What did he say?"

"He said he loved me, of course, that he'd never

loved anyone but me, that just looking at me turned him on, and that he thought the world of Georgia, but that he wasn't attracted to her. He said, you know, that she was a great person but that she was so ugly. Which isn't true, once you know her, but he's a man, and I knew what he meant."

"Yes," said Jane. "But once you know Georgia you forget about it."

"Anyway, I know I made Simon very, very happy in bed, but still that's only a part of love. And I guess he realized that, because eventually we separated, and not long afterwards, Georgia and Simon married. And it was a very happy marriage, Jane. If you were their friend, you must have known that; they were true soul mates. She was so good for him. Simon has this sort of slippery side, where he gets carried away by the illusion of the moment. Georgia was solid and real in a way I never could be. She was perfect for him."

It was a beautiful story, Jane thought. It fit her ideas of Simon and Georgia and her impressions of Ariela. But then, if everything was sweetness and light, why had Pat sent her to talk to Ariela with such dire warnings? What was hidden, or missing in the story? Of course, if Ariela had been unfaithful to Simon very soon after they married, and if he had been completely besotted with her, things must have been much more painful than Ariela's story indicated. Naturally Ariela wouldn't want to think about how she had hurt Simon. But what did that have to do with anything? Could Ariela be lying? Hiding something?

Jane said, "Simon seems to feel very guilty about

Georgia's death. He keeps saying if he had gone home with her, it wouldn't have happened. And Pat said you might . . ."

Ariela put her hands over her face. When she took them away her eyes were wet with tears. "Pat must have guessed, she must have seen us at the party. Oh God. . . ."

"What?"

"Well, the thing is, Simon and I—even after we separated—we still had this powerful effect on each other; I guess in a way we never stopped loving each other. I was at the party, and we were off in the corner talking. . . . We'd had a lot to drink and I'd had a few joints, though, of course, that's no excuse, but we were . . . we couldn't keep our hands off each other. Perhaps Pat saw . . . but I know Georgia couldn't have, because I looked around when I realized how bad we were being and she wasn't in the room then. Anyway, we knew we had to be alone, so we went out to my car . . . to talk, you know . . . but then we made love. Afterwards we both felt terrible. In fact, Simon was sick, literally; he sort of got out of the car and threw up. And I understood what he was feeling, because the trouble was it was always so good between us and that made it worse. So then we went into the house and he couldn't find Georgia and heard she had gone home early. Of course, if she had looked for him, and not been able to find him, and not been able to find me. . . . You can see why Simon is upset. And if he thinks that while we were making love, Georgia met up with her murderer. . . . Oh, poor Simon."

"Poor Simon," Jane echoed, hearing the irony in the words.

"I wish it had never happened," Ariela said. "I feel really bad about it. But at the time we couldn't seem to help it. You know, there was this storm coming on that night, the barometer was very low, and we had this feeling that we were kind of in suspended animation, as if this time we were in together was a kind of island where what happened didn't relate to anything else, didn't count."

"I know. Things like that happen, things you regret later, but can never undo." Jane was trying to comfort Ariela. But the truth was she was shocked and disgusted. She felt hurt for Simon and hurt for Georgia and she wished she had never heard the story. She wasn't sure what connection Pat thought all this had to Georgia's disappearance, but now, all she wanted to do was go home. No, she wanted to see Tom, hold him, and try to get over the feelings of anxiety and disgust that Ariela's story had aroused in her. She felt— she knew—that there was more that she ought to stay and hear, more that she wasn't going to like. But she knew she couldn't deal with any more, so she changed the subject, and soon after she said her goodbyes and left.

Outside, it was dark. The street was quiet and deserted. She phoned Tom from her car and he told her to come right over. Soon she would be lying in his arms, she thought. Tom would comfort her; with him she would be safe.

CHAPTER 17

It had been a beautiful night. Tom had held Jane close and soothed her; they had made love and she awakened in his arms feeling calm and peaceful.

Now it was Saturday and they could have a leisurely morning. The french doors of Tom's kitchen were open to the small city garden and the morning air was soft and spring-like. The day was cloudy, but an occasional ray of sun broke through from time to time, lighting the impatiens in pots on the back terrace and giving the grass a fresh, dewy look. They had spread out *The Globe and Mail* on the kitchen table and were reading it in turn, drawing the other's attention to an article that amused or interested them. Finishing the business section, Tom leaned back with a sigh of pleasure and turned to Jane, smiling. "Feeling better? You look beautiful. You don't seem nearly so tense as you've been the last little while."

She smiled back. "Much, much better. All the same problems are still there, but this morning it seems possible that I could solve them."

"Feel like talking about it?"

"Well, not my problems with the kids. I'm going to meet with the lawyers next week. I've written up a schedule of all the times I tried to get them to stay with me, and I've prepared photocopies of their letters to me. I didn't keep copies of mine to them, though, and if nobody saved them that will be too bad because . . . because I always wrote loving things to them and . . ."

"I know you did, Jane, don't worry, I'm sure your lawyer will sort it out."

"I wish I had your confidence in the legal system. Anyway, let me tell you what Ariela said yesterday, see what you make of it."

Tom listened to Jane's story without interruption, his face hardening as she described what had happened between Simon and Ariela at the party.

"I've met Ariela," he said. "It's true she's beautiful, but she's a dangerous little slut."

"Tom!"

"She comes on to everybody, especially if she thinks you're already taken."

"Don't you think you're being a little unfair? And, anyway, lots of men do that, and no one calls them sluts."

"Well, okay, but even you would have to admit that seducing your ex-husband at a party when his wife—a friend of yours—is there, is sinking pretty low."

"Where do you get the idea that she seduced him?"

"Oh, Jane, come on. It's obvious that's what happened. In fact, I bet, from the way she told you that story, that she and Simon have been seeing each other off and on. That probably wasn't the first time since he married Georgia. His being married to Georgia probably turned her on. Who knows, she's kinky enough to have encouraged him to marry Georgia just for that reason."

"Tom! What are you talking about? Do you know all this or are you just making it up as you go along? And why do you think Simon has no mind of his own?"

He came up behind her and put his arms around her. "I'm not saying Simon isn't at fault, too. You're right about that. But there are women who come on as a challenge and it's something most men just don't know how to deal with; we haven't been trained to say no."

"Give me a break," Jane said. She was upset by the tone Tom was taking. "What's wrong with 'No, I'm married. Thanks anyway.'"

Tom laughed. "Right, you're right. And that's what you say, I take it." He looked at her as he spoke, and she felt herself getting tense as she recognized the look in his eyes, the look that was asking, Have you been faithful? Will you stay faithful? What are you up to? Why can't I trust you?

"Tom," she said gently, "don't you think you are a little paranoid? Maybe the way things worked out with your wife gave you a slanted perspective on women? After all, there are lots of women who don't come on to every man they see, who are faithful and who, when they're weak, are weak because although they want to do the right thing, they get carried away. I mean, we're not all treacherous schemers."

He pulled her up and hugged her, his voice muffled in her hair, "I love you Jane, I truly do." He stepped back and looked at her. "But I still think I'm right about Ariela. I'd bet anything there's a great deal more going on between her and Simon than she says. And I wouldn't be surprised if she wants him back and is trying to get him now that Georgia is out of the picture. I bet financial security looks a lot better to her after she's had a few years on her own. You shouldn't trust her. Don't trust a thing she says to you. Okay? I don't think you're likely to hear the truth from her about Georgia, about Simon, about anything."

Jane turned her head away from Tom and looked out into the garden. The sky, now completely clouded over, was a gentle dove grey. The garden, with its tiny square of neatly mowed grass and its brick terrace and white flowers, looked like an island of perfect serenity. There was no reason, she thought, why her life couldn't be as quiet and calm and peaceful. Maybe she should drop this search into Georgia's past that Simon's guilt and Pat's warnings had drawn her into. She was just risking breaching walls and letting in more pain and unhappiness.

"So what do you think, Jane? Are you going to go on trying to find out what happened to Georgia? Asking for trouble? Asking to find out stuff that makes you miserable?"

She looked back at the garden, savouring it. "Yes, I guess so, I guess I'll go on with it, at least until I understand things a little more."

"But why, Jane? When it makes you so unhappy? That's masochism. Why not let it be?"

"Why? I don't know."

"I was at the party," Tom said. "But I'm sure Pat told you."

Jane turned to look at him, "You were? How come you never mentioned this before?"

"You know we were both invited."

"But you said since I was going to be away you weren't going, that Pat was mostly my friend."

"Well, I changed my mind at the last minute. I was feeling kind of lonely, with you away. . . . I thought for sure Pat would have told you."

"I can't believe this. Did you see Georgia?"

"That's what I'm trying to tell you. I turned up early, and there was no one there I knew. It didn't seem like a very good party, so I had a few drinks and took off. Ask anybody. I only stayed an hour or so."

Jane thought Tom's tone was peculiar, his expression was peculiar. There was something about his story she couldn't understand. But she didn't feel like pushing him. She could tell that if she did, he would get angry and their day together would be ruined and he still wouldn't tell her. She'd just have to find out some other way. The thought made her uneasy; she sensed that when she did come to understand what was behind his strange manner, she wasn't going to like it at all.

CHAPTER 18

Jane liked Sgt Barrodale, of the Metropolitan
Toronto Police Serious Crimes Division, and she
thought he liked her. Although, in their previous
encounter, it was Jane who had figured out who
had committed the crime she had become
enmeshed in, it was the police who had gathered
the evidence that led to the conviction. Jane had
never imagined that she was a detective or a solver
of crimes; she believed that she was more than willing to hand over to the police everything she knew
or suspected, even when it seemed to tell against
people she cared for, confident that the police
would sort through it and no serious harm would
be done.

Jane's best friend, Kersti, a journalist, had
warned her that this attitude was hopelessly naïve,
but Jane, so far, had had no reason to change her
mind. Now sitting across from Sgt Barrodale, smiling at him, she hoped that he would remember
her past helpfulness and tell her what she wanted
to know about Georgia's death.

"Is it your case now?" she asked him, watching

143

him push aside a pile of file folders, an evidence box, and a sheaf of memos to make room for the printouts she had brought him.

Sgt Barrodale was a big, bulky man with thinning blond hair, grown long at the sides and combed over a widening bald spot in an ineffective but endearing effort to cover it. He had mild blue eyes and a deceptively incurious, placid, and rather unintelligent air. Jane had accepted this manner was one of many; she guessed that with her he adopted the persona he used to meet the public when they were of the hard-working, lawabiding and probably extremely well-connected middle and upper-middle classes. From time to time she caught glimpses of other less likeable Sgt Barrodales: the tough cop, the right-wing law enforcement officer, the meticulous investigator, the bullier of recalcitrant suspects. Rather than causing her concern, these other Barrodales only made him more real and likeable to her; God knew there were enough contradictory Jane Tregars inside her.

"My case?" He smiled and patted his breast pocket, found a package of cigarettes, took them out, removed one from the packet and waved it at her. She nodded and he lit up. "For the moment. And I probably have you to thank for that."

"Me?"

"According to what we found in our preliminary investigation, you know just about everyone likely to be involved. The original officers on the case thought you could be a big help. So, since I knew you, it seemed like a good idea to put me on the team."

"That's great," Jane said. "I'll be glad to answer any questions you have if you'll tell me what happened, how the investigation's going, stuff like that."

"Now, Jane, you remember it doesn't work like that. You tell us what you know—"

"Okay, okay, I understand you have to say that."

After some more preliminary jockeying for position, Sgt Barrodale agreed to give Jane the "background." He told her that according to the report from forensic pathology, Georgia had died around the time of the party. In fact, the pathologist's report, combined with the police investigation of Georgia's last day, suggested that she probably met her death some time between five and ten o'clock the evening of the party. Her last meal appeared to be lunch the day of the party and she had consumed some drinks later in the day, soon before her death, suggesting that she might have arrived at the party, had a few drinks, left and been killed soon after leaving. Although it was also possible, Barrodale pointed out, that Georgia had left the party and had a drink or two elsewhere. Sgt Barrodale told Jane that Georgia had not been killed at the place where she was found. Death had occurred somewhere else; the body had been left to lie in one position for some time—hours, maybe days—then it had been moved to the woods where it was found. The murderer had hidden Georgia so well that finding her had been

most unlikely; it was a fluke that young boys playing had stumbled into that particular thorny
blackberry bramble and found her body.

Georgia had been strangled, not with a rope or
fabric, but by a pair of hands. But the depreda-
tions of animals had made it impossible to be sure
with how much force, or to check for the marks of
fingernails, or get a sense of the hand span of the
strangler.

Jane swallowed and tried to control the rush of
emotions that threatened to overtake her as she
heard her friend Georgia described as a "body" to
whom dreadful things had happened. "Do you
think she suffered much? Was there any sign that
she was . . . molested? Any evidence that she was
kidnapped or held, anything like that?"

"The physical evidence is poor. It was hot, she
was in the woods where there are many small animals, insects; nature takes its course when the
dead are left lying for three weeks—you have to
understand that." He looked at her, checking, she
thought, to be sure she could handle what he was
telling her.

She managed a smile to reassure him that she
could accept what she was hearing. "Anything else?
What was she wearing? The same clothes she wore
to the party?"

"According to her husband, she was. It would be
nice to have that confirmed. But so far we haven't
talked to anyone at the party who remembered what
she was wearing. That's not surprising, you know.
The party was some time ago and I think there was
a lot of drinking going on. In one case, or two,

people thought they remembered, but it turned out they were mixing up previous encounters with Georgia with this one. I gather she was a memorable woman, more for her personality than her appearance."

Jane nodded. "What else?"

"Well, let's see." In an involuntary gesture he loosened his tie. Jane imagined he had put one on for his appointment with her, as it seemed not to suit him. He wore a crumpled beige summer-weight suit, made of some synthetic that showed both creases and the slightly fuzzy look acrylics get as they age. His tie, a blue knit, was not nearly long enough to cover the hard round stomach, which strained buttons of his shirt. He had undone his jacket soon after sitting down behind his desk. "The way we see it, there are two possibilities. One, she was killed by someone she didn't know, a crazy she met up with after she left the party. Two, she was killed by someone she knew. We're leaning that way."

"Why?"

"Because there was such a big effort made to hide her identity. Everything that might have helped to identify her had been removed and hidden. That's not usual in cases where the perpetrator is unknown to the victim."

"Oh."

"Right now, the way we see it, most of our prime suspects were at that party. But we aren't getting much information to help us narrow the field. Nobody remembers when she left, no one knows if she left alone, no one had any reason to want her dead, etcetera."

"So what do you think?"

"You really want to know? The truth is right now the investigation is going nowhere. Naturally we've talked to her husband, Simon Arnott. We tend to check out the spouse first in a case like this. He seems very cut up by her death, and at the moment I have no reason to doubt him. He didn't inherit any money or benefit by her death; everyone said they got along great. They'd only been married a couple of years and they seemed to have a pretty good marriage.

"At work, she'd had some run-ins with some of her co-workers. We've read her project diary; she'd had trouble with this Ivor, with Red Kieran and with Catherine Brooks. But nothing very serious, from the sounds of it. Or, at least, she didn't think so.

"Malcolm Morton, her boss, was depending on her to get a new product out. Her death is bad news for him. And Morton wasn't at the party, though, of course, he has a house within walking distance and he was at home that night. As for Arnott's ex-wife, she divorced him, not the other way around, so it's hard to see any reason for her to do it. Anyway, she seems to have more than enough current lovers to keep her from wanting Arnott back. Best reason of all for putting her at the bottom of the list, several people remember both Arnott and his ex-wife were still at the party after Georgia left."

"You're accepting the assumption that she was murdered soon after she left the party?"

"We're working on that basis." He had put his cigarette in an aluminum disposable ashtray, and a thin column of smoke ascended towards the air outtake vent, filling the room with its scent, so that Jane was slightly nauseated. She refrained from asking him to put it out, not wanting to stop the flow of information. He took a puff, looked at her, smiled his small, serious smile, stubbed it out, leaned back in his chair, locked his arms behind his head, and watched her with his mild, steady gaze.

"The husband went home after the party with Ivor," Sgt Barrodale said, not taking his eyes from Jane's face. "The story is that Ivor wanted to talk to Georgia at the party, to apologize about something or other. But he drank too much and forgot to do it. Arnott says he agreed to give Ivor a lift into the city; they thought Ivor could talk to Georgia, sleep over and then take the subway home in the morning—of course it would be shut down by the time they got to Toronto.

"But when they arrived at the Arnotts' she wasn't there, and she didn't turn up in the morning. And there was no sign that she'd come home either. You know, porch light not on, alarm still set. Arnott said he could tell from looking at the bathroom that she hadn't been there. He said the towels were untouched and all the lights off. Best as Arnott could figure it, she never came home. So for now we're thinking she must have either left the party with her attacker or met him outside Pat Hornby's house, and gone off with him either willingly or unwillingly. And was killed soon after."

"Have you followed up on that?"

"Yes, but so far nothing. After all, that party was out in the country. Everyone got there by car and went home that way. The couples all account for each other, whatever that means. A lot of the singles car-pooled, so one could stay relatively sober and the others drink, or so they told me." He smiled again, a bleak, disbelieving smile. "But from a practical point of view, their stories are reasonable and check out as well as can be expected."

"So, where do you go from here?"

"That's why I wanted to talk to you, Jane. We're going to have to check out the alibis for everybody at that party a lot more deeply. I'd like to use my resources as efficiently as possible, concentrate on the most likely suspects, you know. I think you could save me a great deal of time."

"How's that?"

"Come on, Jane, you know what I'm getting at. Here." He slid a typed list across the desk towards her. "This is everyone who was at the party. Plus Morton; he was at home alone that night. You probably know most of them. You know Georgia. You're working at her desk. In a sense you're wearing her shoes." Jane shuddered. "The hostility, the problems she had at work—you've probably got a good feel for them. You know her husband, her boss. How about giving me your take on this list? It could be a big help."

Jane picked up the list and ran her eyes down the columns of names. How bizarre it felt to look over a list of people, most of whom she knew, and ask herself who might have been likely to strangle one of the best people she had ever known. There was an unreal repellent quality to it. Of course, none of them could possibly have done such a thing. She threw the list down on the desk. Sgt Barrodale said nothing. On the other hand, she thought, any of them could have done it. Within herself, weren't there repulsive depths, rages, ugly things? Why should these people be any different? She picked up the list again. Someone had killed Georgia, she reminded herself. If it was someone on the list, then she wanted that person found out. She looked up at Barrodale. "Wouldn't it have to be someone very strong? Georgia was a tall woman and she seemed quite fit. Surely someone small and relatively weak—my size say—couldn't harm a person like Georgia."

"You're probably right, but we can't count on that. If someone she trusted came close to her, surprised her . . . it's hard to say."

"But not a woman," Jane said, thinking without wanting to of Ariela, of Ariela's leaning towards her in greeting, drawing Jane into her living-room with that caressing, firm grasp.

"Women greet each other with kisses on the cheek, they hug in parting; at least, these kind of people often do," Sgt Barrodale said. "Maybe a woman leaned over to give her a kiss on the cheek and then strangled her before she was aware of what was happening. It would be better not to assume anything at this stage. Just tell me who on that list you think we can cross off, who you think deserves more attention."

"God, I don't know." Jane got up, walked over

the window, looked out without seeing anything, came back to her chair, sat down and took a pencil out of a container full of them. "Here," she said, "I'm ticking off the people I don't know. And these names I'm putting X's next to, as far as I know, weren't close to Georgia." She came to Tom's name and wondered, again, why he had been so unwilling to talk about the party, so late in telling her he had gone. But what difference could it make? He had left early, before Georgia got there. "Of course, my thinking they hardly knew Georgia, that means nothing. They might have been fast friends without my being aware of it. She steeled herself. "Like Tom, the man I live with, he knows Simon, a little, because of business connections, but he doesn't really know Georgia, except through me."

He smiled his sad little smile at her, the one that seemed to say that she had passed a test. "Yes, right. But you don't need to worry about Tom. Even if he did know her better than you think, he's not a suspect. Several people told us he left very early, before the Arnotts got there."

"I wasn't worrying," Jane said untruthfully. In fact, it was a great relief to hear that Barrodale believed Tom was out of the picture. Finding this out was one of her main reasons for meeting with Barrodale, but she had not known how to ask. She was happy to change the subject. "Have you asked Simon do this too, to go over a list and mark out the most likely suspects?"

Barrodale nodded.

"Good, then I don't feel quite so scummy. Now

here, I'm putting little question marks next to the people who were close enough to Georgia, so that she was important in their lives."

She finished marking the list and passed it over the desk to him, then looked down at her hands crossed on her lap, noticing, not for the first time, how, in the past few years, the skin had become slightly freckled and marked by the faintest of lines between the base of her thumb and her wrists. Each year left its subtle traces, she thought, but where is the wisdom that was supposed to justify this downward path? She hadn't seen any signs of it.

Sgt Barrodale's voice intruded into her thoughts. "I see you've put question marks by the obvious ones: Malcolm Morton, Ivor, Red and Catherine. That makes sense. But you've also marked Ariela, the ex-wife. Why is that?"

"I'm not sure," Jane lied, finding herself unable to repeat Ariela's story about her and Simon's behaviour at the party, though she knew it was something she really ought to tell Barrodale. "I went to talk to her about Georgia, and she had only nice things to say about her. She even said that, when her marriage to Simon was falling apart, she kind of pushed him at Georgia, told him to marry her."

"That might well be true," Barrodale said. "Arnott told me the same thing."

"Did he? Knowing she was telling me the truth about that makes me feel a little better about her. Still, it's a condescending kind of thing to do. But the truth of it is"—I wonder, Jane thought, why I

say "the truth of it" when I'm not sure I'm telling
the truth—"the truth of it is, I don't exactly trust
her. Maybe that's because of some nasty things
Tom said about her. I think he knows her and he
doesn't trust her. Anyway, better safe than sorry,
right?"

"That's how we see it. So . . . you've got Ivor,
Red, Malcolm, Ariela, Catherine. But not Simon
or Pat?"

"Pat? Well, they knew each other professionally,
but they weren't close enough to matter to each
other." Even as she spoke, she was thinking of Pat's
curious behaviour. Pat had described a professional relationship with Ariela that had once been
close and then had become less so, without giving
any reason for the estrangement. Pat had warned
her not to look into Georgia's death and wouldn't
say why. There was something peculiar there, no
doubt about it. But whatever it was, it most likely
had to do with Ariela, not Georgia.

"I think you can forget Pat. There just isn't
enough connection between her life and
Georgia's. As for Simon . . . I know husbands are
popular suspects. But he pleaded with me to find
out what happened to her. And he's really suffering over her death. He's falling apart; you have
only to look at him."

Barrodale smiled. This time, it seemed to Jane,
it was an even sadder smile than before, mocking
and sarcastic. "You'd be surprised what I see in this
job," he said. "If you want to leave him off because
he's heart-broken, I'd advise you not to. But his
asking you to find out what happened to her . . .

now that, that's strange."

"Strange?" said Jane, stung. "What do you mean 'strange'? Didn't I figure out who murdered Gary Levin at BTS? Simon knew that. Why shouldn't he believe I could help?"

"Right. No offence meant. We'll buy it at the price you're selling it. Anyway, there are better reasons to cross him off the suspect list." He smiled at her again, this time with warmth. "If anyone in this whole bunch has an alibi, it's him. He left the party after his wife did, with Ivor. Ivor spent the night at his house, in a room above the driveway. If Simon had driven out that night, Ivor would have heard. The next day Arnott was going round to her friends looking for Georgia. Almost all his time's accounted for. So unless someone else snatched her and he polished her off, he's most likely in the clear. At the moment I'd put my money on Ivor, Morton, Pat, Catherine and Ariela, if you want to include her, as the most likely suspects. Comment?"

Suddenly, Jane couldn't take it any more. Sgt Barrodale sitting there, calmly assessing the likelihood that one of five people, all of whom she knew, might have murdered one of her dearest friends, was more than she could bear. She stood up abruptly, picked up her purse and stretched out her hand to Barrodale. "I'm sorry, I have to go now. Really. I'll get back to you if I think of anything that might be helpful to you."

"Jane," he said, rising from his chair and coming around the side of his desk, looking down at her, making her feel suddenly very small and very cowardly, "Jane, I thought we agreed. . . ."

"Yes, we did, and I will help, you'll see. I promise. I'll get back to you, it's just that, seeing that list of my friends, of people I know, talking about them as suspects—it's enough for today, okay?"

"I understand." He walked with her down the hall, into the lobby of the Serious Crimes Division, out the double-glass doors to the elevator. "I understand how you feel about this, Jane, but I do need your help. We're not getting anywhere, and your knowledge of these people could be a big help to the investigation. Believe me, we're counting on you. Someone murdered your friend. If you can help us, you should."

"I know."

"That's right, Jane. You know. I think you know more than you're saying, more than you're admitting yourself. When we last worked together you were calm and rational. Now you seem emotional, involved. What's the matter? What aren't you telling me?"

"Involved?" She jabbed the elevator button. "Involved? No way. All I care about is finding out what happened to Georgia."

The elevator arrived and the doors slid open. It was empty and Jane stepped in, turning to face Barrodale, who stood in the hallway looking at her with a puzzled, doubtful expression on his face. She looked back at him, met his perceptive, measuring gaze. "When I know something for sure, I'll tell you," she said. Then, feeling again that strange mixture of longing to know the truth about what had happened and dread over what she might find out, she said, defensively, "Don't look at me like that. I want to know what happened to Georgia as much as you do."

"Is that right?" said Sgt Barrodale, and as the elevator door closed Jane saw he was smiling his sad, knowing smile.

CHAPTER 19

In Jane's office Ivor was pacing back and forth, while Red and Catherine, seated on the visitors' chairs opposite Jane's desk, were looking at her with angry, stubborn expressions.

"Let's face it, Jane, what do you know about software development, I mean, really," Ivor said. "So you've written the odd C program in your youth, or whatever. This is an entirely different realm we're in. You're just going to have to take my word for it, and Catherine's. The fact is Crystal is not ready, and it's not going to be ready. The release date will have to be postponed. And that's it!"

"We can't let it go without these fixes," Catherine said. "We'll be the laughing stock of the industry."

"I'm really steamed about this," Red said, angrily tugging at his beard. "It's just so dumb! After all this work—to blow it at the last minute!"

"It's going out," Jane said. "I say, so, Malcolm says so. Georgia thought it was ready. That's good enough."

"Georgia! Well she's gone now, let's face it. What

she thought isn't worth a mashed potato," Ivor said, coming back to the desk and sitting down. "We're the experts here. We know when a product is ready for release and when it's not."

"Two hundred and seventy-four bugs from the Arco field test!" Red said.

"None of those bugs were true bugs, according to Georgia's definitions, you know that," Jane said calmly. "I've studied the bug reports, and I've decided that—"

"You've decided, *you've* decided—that's the point!" Ivor said. "You don't . . ."

Malcolm Morton opened the door. "Am I interrupting a good fight?" he said, smiling.

"Malcolm! Just the man," Red said, jumping up and waving Malcolm to sit down in his chair. "It's about the release date. We're telling Jane, no way."

"Prospero is going to lay one giant egg if we release Crystal now," Ivor said, walking over to the wall to stand beside Red.

Malcolm sat down and leaned back, stretching his legs out in front of him. He looked at Ivor, Red and Catherine in turn, taking in their flushed faces, their angry expressions. "Jane has already discussed this with me," he said. "And we have agreed. There will be no delay. The issues raised in the field test will be dealt with in the next release. The product is going out on time. Discussion closed." He stood up, turned so his face was hidden from the three of them, and winked at Jane. She started.

"Just a minute, Malcolm," Catherine said. Her

voice had a cold, detached tone. "We have our professional reputations to think of; there's a point past which we can't be pushed. And if all of us agree, unanimously, I think our views deserve more consideration then a flat turn down. You haven't even listened to our point of view. You owe us that, after all we've put into Crystal."

"Do I?" Malcolm said. "Well, maybe I do and maybe I don't. But right now you all seem to me to be too heated up to deal with this rationally. Why don't you leave Jane and me, I have some other matters to talk over with her. And if I decide to reopen the question, we'll call a meeting for this afternoon, say 4:00 P.M.?"

After he had followed them to the door and shut it behind them, Malcolm came back and sat down in front of Jane's desk. "Well, you seem calm enough for someone who is being beaten up three on one."

Jane smiled. "I'm not really calm, but when people lose their temper like that, it just gets my back up. I don't like to see them get away with it."

"Good for you. They did the same thing to Georgia off and on during the development of Crystal. She told me it's pretty common for people like Ivor, Red and Catherine to have a dread of seeing their work go out the door."

"That's right. And of course, in a way, everything they say is true. Another six months in the lab, and Crystal would be a much better product. But, as I understand it, we don't have six months. Our market window is now, right? And I've seen the results of the tests. It's good enough."

"Are you sure, Jane?"

"No, of course I'm not sure. It's just my best guess, that's all."

"I'm not doubting your judgment. I just want you to assure me that you've thought it through from every angle and aren't saying that because Georgia thought so. Things change very fast in this business, and I know I don't need to remind you that there's a lot riding on this release—the future of Prospero, millions of dollars of my money and the jobs of eighty people."

"Prospero has other products. It's not going to go under if this one fails, is it?"

"It is. Prospero has been losing money for the past few years, and I'll put it into receivership or fold it into something else and let most of the people go rather than keep pouring money into a sink-hole. Do you want to think again? A delay of a month, two months—"

"No!"

"Remember, just because Georgia said release this fall, it doesn't mean that's written in blood."

."It's tied in with the whole marketing plan, Malcolm. You'll lose a couple of hundred thousand already committed, and you'll lose the backing of the dealers and all the support training we've done. And you'll seriously harm the credibility of Crystal."

"Okay, but how do you plan to handle those three? We need them—Catherine with her Ph.D. in linguistics, Ivor with his experience in AI at

Carnegie Mellon, and Red as the top programmer—having them identified with Crystal is critical for the trade."

"I know. I was thinking I'd talk to them each separately. It's impossible when they're together. The thing is," Jane said, running her hand through her hair and pressing her fingers down on her scalp, "this resistance of theirs isn't rational."

"That's my sense, too," Malcolm said. "After all, if they believed the commercial arguments, they'd want it out on time. To be sure they gave us every ounce, Georgia recommended I give them stock in the company and now they've all got options. If we succeed with Crystal and go public, they should do very well."

"If that's true," Jane said thoughtfully, smoothing her hair back into place, "then their resistance to Crystal going out on time gets even harder to understand. You're right; I could understand mixed motives. Wanting it out so they could make the money they're counting on . . . and not wanting it out in case it isn't as good as advertised, or their peers find fault. But they seem pretty unanimously opposed."

"Then maybe there are more problems than you realize," Malcolm said.

"I suppose I ought to look deeper. I hate to think about what all this might mean," Jane said grudgingly, feeling anxious, as his questions unsettled the certainty that the temper tantrums of the development team had failed to sway. "But Georgia was so confident that it was ready—and that was weeks ago."

"Something new from the field tests?"

"No. I've gone over the reports with a fine-tooth comb. I even went over to Arco and talked to people there. They loved Crystal, just loved it. The problems they identified aren't problems, they're a wish list for future features. Just as Georgia predicted. I'm starting to get a bad feeling about all of this; I hope I'm wrong." There was a silence while both mulled over the implications of what they were saying.

"What are you thinking, Jane?" Malcolm leaned forward, looking at her intently. Jane was aware of how good-looking he was. The problem is, she thought, though I try not to notice, when we're talking as equals, working closely together, when we're allies facing a problem, I find that erotic. Not very smart. It also wouldn't be very smart to tell him my fears about industrial espionage, she thought. She had no proof, and no executive likes to hear his manager bad-mouthing the people who work under her.

"I'm thinking something I'd rather not discuss until I have some evidence."

"You can't just leave it at that."

"I don't want to suggest—"

"Consider yourself ordered to suggest whatever it is you're worrying about. I need to know."

"Well . . . if that's an order."

They smiled at one another.

"I hope you'll tell me that what's on my mind is impossible. Ivor is always saying how the three of them *are* Crystal. I think he believes it, believes they could do it pretty well on their own. Suppose they've lost confidence in Prospero. You're talking about receivership if it doesn't succeed. With my taking Georgia's place, maybe they think they're never going to see the windfall profits they'd get if Prospero went public." She spoke very softly, averting her face from his steady gaze. "Maybe they're negotiating with a competitor. They'll bring him the technology, help him launch a competitive product. Of course, there'd be legal problems, but they might be able to get away with it. If that's what's going on, the longer they stall Crystal, the better for them." She raised her hand, palm out, as if pushing the idea away. "I have no reason to think this, none at all, but working for Orloff has given me a suspicious mind."

"I like that suspicious mind, Jane. True or not, we need to check it out. Can you do that?"

"I can try. I'll call around, see if anybody is talking about a similar product anywhere, under development, about to be released, whatever. I have lots of friends in the industry; I'll see what I can find out. We don't want to destroy what's left of our team spirit if I'm wrong."

"Sounds good. Get on with it." He leaned back in his chair, smiling slightly. "And, on another topic, are you and Tom doing anything this weekend? I was hoping to convince you to come out to the farm. I've bought some new horses, just for riding, not racing. I thought you'd like to try them out."

"Tom's away for the next two weeks on business. And he isn't interested in horses anyway."

"Well, why don't you come then? We'll have a

chance to bat these problems around with the pressure off, and see what we can come up with. And there's nothing like a good horse to take your mind off your business worries."

"That would be wonderful," Jane said. "But I don't think Tom would appreciate my staying with you alone. How about if I stay with Pat?"

"Sure. Good idea. But I'll expect you for a late supper on Friday. About eight or eight-thirty. And don't bring Pat. Seeing my ex, fond as I am of her, isn't my idea of a relaxing weekend. Okay?"

"I'd love it," Jane said truthfully. "A weekend in the country, away from all this. And to get your ideas about the things that have been worrying me here . . . that would be really great." They smiled at one another.

But after Malcolm left, Jane felt her pleasure drain away. What was she up to to agree to a week-end riding and talking with Malcolm? Was the smile he had given her as business-like as they were both pretending? But if not, so what? She knew that she had no intention of getting involved with Malcolm. There was Tom, of course. And even if he weren't in the picture, it would be a big mistake—getting mixed up with her employer—one she couldn't afford to make.

She had enough problems without that one.

CHAPTER 20

Jane had been calling around to contacts of hers, trying to find out if anyone had heard about a product like Crystal being developed by another software firm, or if there was any indication that Ivor, Red and Catherine had been talking to a competitor. She had spoken to about a third of the names on her list when her lawyer's call came through.

"Good news, Jane," he said. His voice had a heavier note of irony than usual. "At least I think it is. It looks like we were right—the business of the kids getting their own lawyer and suing to stay with their father was a ploy. I guess they were waiting until we were suitably softened up, because today I got a call from Bernie's lawyer. They're offering us an out-of-court settlement."

Jane stared out at the parking lot. What was Bernie up to now? She had lost any trust she might once have had in him. What a downward cycle it had been. What had become of the naïve, idealistic girl of nineteen who had fallen in love with the sophisticated Swiss financier? After two years of

166

marriage that girl was gone, replaced by an inexperienced young woman trapped in a marriage with an older, autocratic man from a different culture whose expectations she could never meet. Bernie had believed there was only one way Jane could be a good wife and mother. As he saw it, he had made a contract with her; he intended to keep his side of the bargain and expected her to do the same. When he decided she was incapable of her part, he had considered the contract breached. Sometimes she wondered if the woman she was now would have the capacity to keep Bernie happy, look after his houses and children and still remain whole. But of course, it was a foolish question. The woman she was now would never have married Bernie.

It was a mistake from which she could never recover, because, although the marriage was over, the children she loved and wanted were his. To play any part in their lives she had to do battle with a clever, manipulative father who had created a home for his children and slowly gained control over their lives, while denigrating hers. Through it all, he had been gentlemanly, considerate, had held back from doing anything more than he had to, as long as he was in control. But once she had threatened that control by suing him for custody of the children, the rules had changed. Now, she had discovered, she was in a battle, just like a business battle, where money, strategic intelligence, power and connections were the critical cards. And because her emotions were too near the surface, too strong to control, she feared she was going to lose. It was a game she was teaching herself to play at work, but it was far from mastered. She didn't think she was going to be able to rise to the challenge when the stakes were her own children. The ache of missing them clouded her judgment, preventing her from being able to bluff or take any risks with what meant more to her than anything else. Her lawyer had warned her time and time again that it was crucial for her to maintain her objectivity and composure if they were to win.

"He's offered to drop the suit and to accept joint custody."

"What? I don't believe it! Where's the catch?"

"You're right, there's a catch. It's his definition of joint custody. You get to see the children as often as you want—if you join them in their homes in either Toronto, the south of France or Lausanne. You can stay with the family and visit with the children, 'in the manner of a relative,' is the way they phrase it. But you can't take the kids from the family home for more than an hour, and when you do you must be accompanied by either your ex-husband, his wife or the children's au pair."

"What's that? Why, that's outrageous!"

"Your husband's lawyer explained that they think this is a win-win proposal. You can see the children as much as you want, they can get to know you, yet your husband will never have to fear that you might abduct them or try to undo their 'primary upbringing.'"

"I don't believe this. Abduct them! He's the one

who is always threatening to take them away to Switzerland! Live with Bernie and Madeleine! Even for a day, how could I agree to something like that? I would become the kids' aunt, or something. I'm their mother for God's sake!"

"Now just calm down. Remember what I told you: they're negotiators. If this makes you see red, then I would guess your husband foresaw that—it's part of his plan."

"Oh God, you're right. Of course. He's doing this to make me back off."

"So, do I take it from your reaction that the answer is no?"

"Of course the answer is no!"

"Jane, you should consider this. You shouldn't just react without thinking it through. We need to think how to reply. We can't just turn it down and have it on record that we wouldn't consider what appears, on the face of it, to be a reasonable offer. Open access, any time, plus virtually free room and board for you in Toronto, Lausanne or the south of France."

"You can't be serious! Any judge would see that those conditions would be intolerable for an ex-wife!"

"In custody battles, Jane, the court tries to decide what is best for the children, not for the parents."

"It would be intolerable for the children!"

"So you say, and I hear you. I still think you need to mull this over and give me a more thought-out response. How about I call you next week. Take the weekend to think about it. Will you do that, Jane?"

Jane knew he was right. They needed a better
response, a more creative response, than a cry of
outrage and hurt. She managed to get her voice
under control and agreed to the suggestion. But
when she hung up, got herself a coffee, drank it,
and returned to her list, she found that the zest
with which she had been looking forward to
uncovering the motives of Ivor, Red and Catherine
had vanished, to be replaced with a flat, calm kind
of sadness. What did it matter, really, if Ivor and
company were planning to ditch Prospero and
jump ship to another company? They'd left it too
late to really hurt Crystal. Crystal was ready; a few
last-minute fixes, tune up the documentation and
packaging, and they would be all set for product
release. The three of them would look like real
opportunists if they went to a competitor at this
stage.

But could that be what had happened? That
they had thought, with Jane replacing Georgia,
they could stall the release long enough to give the
competitors a chance? And now they were panick-
ing?

She got up abruptly and headed for Ivor's
office.

"I'd like to understand," Jane said, looking at
Ivor, unsmiling, "why, when you have enough stake
in Prospero to have a lot to lose if Crystal misses its
release date, you are working so hard to delay it?"

Ivor's office was as neat as a pin. He had three
computers: two different PC's, each one running a
different operating system, and a Sun workstation.
All three were connected by a Local Area Network

to Prospero's mini-computer. His shelves were full of technical journals, neatly organized by date, and binders of computer and software documentation. On his desk there was nothing but a stack of printouts, covered with jottings in red ink. Now he pulled off his glasses and rubbed his eyes wearily. Then he ran his fingers through his short, wiry dark beard. He drummed them on the shiny top of his desk. "First, I want to apologize for leading that guerrilla assault on you this morning. It was a stupid thing to do, and I'm sorry."

"It's not so much what you did, it's why."

"Take a chair, Jane. Let's talk."

Ivor's desk was pushed up against the wall in the corner of his office. It was L-shaped; one arm being a proper desk with drawers, the other a table on a lower level, on which were the three computers. A single visitor chair had been placed at the end of the desk part of the L. When Jane sat down, Ivor swivelled his chair so he was facing her, his knees only a few inches from hers, his face now at eye-level and very close. She could see the enlarged pores in his cheeks and his curiously beautiful eyes. They were very large, with long dark lashes, the whites slightly yellowed, the irises almost black. He was looking at her intently and because his eyes looked so directly at her, there was a seductive quality to the look, which Jane had to resist with an effort. It was as if, she thought, he was consciously trying to exercise power over her. She had observed him dominating Red and Catherine, who were both strong personalities. Even Malcolm had had to make an effort to assert himself against Ivor when there was a disagreement. Ivor's power lay partly in the potent quality of his extraordinary intelligence and wilfulness, and Jane realized that she was afraid of him. She felt a very strong impulse to back her chair away, to widen the space between them, but she resisted.

"First of all," he said smiling, "let me say I'm glad you asked that question. I'd like to get some of this stuff out in the open. We're all under such pressure; I know sometimes we don't take the time we should to explain things. We just rant and rave and try to stomp on whoever's in our way. I think we've been doing that with you, and I'm sorry. To answer your question: Yes, we all have share options in Prospero. We want Crystal to succeed. That's exactly why we're trying to delay it. We know it will bomb if it comes out before it's ready."

"And you know that's not necessarily so. Malcolm has said he'll put Prospero into receivership if it doesn't start making a profit this year. Crystal has to be released next month."

"Trust me. I've had a lot more experience with new software products than you have. I've had lots more experience with the Malcolm Mortons of this world. Crystal is going to be big—giant. Prospero is going to make millions, maybe hundreds of millions, off it. Products like Crystal come along only once in a generation. You had MS-DOS, you had Lotus 1-2-3 and Dbase-3, now you have Crystal. Crystal is going to mean that anybody who knows zilch about computers can use any computer with Crystal on it, without having to remember a damn thing about it. Plus the natural language-smart help-on-a-chip is going to be a necessity for every new software program that runs on a machine that doesn't have Crystal. We're going to get them coming and going. So I ask you, is Malcolm going to walk away from that because of a delay of a few months? The hell he is."

Not for the first time since coming to Prospero, Jane felt her certainty challenged. "Then why was Georgia so adamant that it had to go out on schedule?"

"Why? I don't know why. But I can guess. You want my guesses?"

"Of course."

He rolled his chair back slightly, widening the space between them. He drummed his fingers on the desk, giving Jane the impression that he had better things to do with his time than explain simple things to her. Jane found the dry thumping noise his fingers made extremely irritating.

"Georgia was an unusual person, I don't have to tell you that. She was smart, no doubt about that. Brilliant actually. Just about one of the smartest people I ever met—but limited. Because Georgia played by the rules. She learned the rules for everything, and then she followed them. Georgia had a Ph.D. in computer science, but she never did a single innovative piece of programming. Everything she did was an elaboration of someone else's work. She didn't take risks; she didn't solve hard problems. She used her intelligence to figure out how things worked, how they got done; then, she made things that were in trouble work and she got things that weren't getting done, done. She had a library of solutions in her head, orders of magnitude bigger than anyone else I've ever met, but they were all solutions created by someone else."

"Well, I knew her, and I don't agree. But for the sake of argument, suppose you're right. What's the point?"

"The point is no software product that has missed its window has succeeded. Software products that are delayed and delayed usually bomb. That's the basis of Georgia's certainty, and nobody and nothing could sway her from that. But you're not like that, Jane. You're just the opposite from Georgia, as far as I can tell. Not in intelligence," he said smiling. "I'm not saying you're not smart. But I mean, as far as I can see, you operate by intuition. You look over the surface of things and then you have this amazing ability to see the main points and put things together in new ways. It's great. We all admire you, we think it's astonishing how fast you've picked up what we're doing without really understanding anything."

Jane accepted this left-handed compliment with a sour little smile. She hated being told she operated by intuition. It was so often what men said about women whose actions they didn't agree with.

"We think you're doing a great job. We've told Malcolm we think that. He's asked us if he should try to get you to stay on, rather than find a replacement. Of course, he has a problem there; it's got to be hard to find someone who's willing to take on the job of project manager at the tail-end of a project. You might be the solution. But the trouble with you is this incredible, irrational loyalty to Georgia. Georgia said this, Georgia did that, so you think you have to stand by it. Don't! Go with your own intuition."

"I'm not backing a fall product release because Georgia believed it was right," Jane said stiffly. "It's because I think so. That's my judgment."

"Is that true? Think about it. Do you honestly want to go against the best judgment of Red, Catherine and me? People who want nothing more in this whole God-damned world than to see Crystal succeed? People who together have thirty years of experience in this? Come on, Jane. It just doesn't make sense."

His hypnotic eyes were on her again, flattering yet insistent; she could feel the power of his personality. She felt diminished and flattened. But, as always with her, pressure, the urging of people who tried to overpower her, incited only resistance. A desire to strike back, to make more equal the contending forces, so that the argument or discussion could be between two equals rather than between active strength and passive acceptance.

"I understand everything you are saying, Ivor, and I have a great deal of respect for it. But you have to remember that I listen to the other side from the marketing people. And I have a great deal of respect for them too. It's true you three have thirty years of experience in software development. But the marketing team has the expertise in when to go to market, in that timing. And—"

"And you believe that in a battle between technical and marketing, marketing ought to win. Damn it, Jane, that's stupid. It's just God-damn stupid! Don't think that way. Don't screw up the product of the century so some salesman can get his commission this year!"

"Georgia—"

"There you go! Jesus Christ. What Georgia thought isn't worth a smartie in a hellhole to anyone. She's dead. She's history, Jane. Forget her. She was wrong when she was here. She was wrecking this project. Now we have a chance to win. So think for yourself. Let go of Georgia. She wasn't perfect. She was wrong—very, very wrong. And now she's dead. Okay? Face it, Jane. Georgia is dead. And this is up to you."

CHAPTER 21

Without his colleagues to buttress him, Red was meek, almost apologetic. Sitting across from him, in his office, Jane was struck by the way he compressed his mouth into a thin, tight line, as if forcing himself towards a toughness unnatural to him. Remembering the volatile temper he had shown whenever he was under pressure, his lack of finesse in dealing with people, she was not at all surprised that Ivor dominated him so easily.

Now, seeing her cold and unsmiling face, he slouched back in his chair, nervously scratched his unkempt reddish beard, tugged at his ears, rubbed his eyes, and frequently passed his hands over his mouth. "Of course I want Crystal to succeed. Why wouldn't I?"

Jane repeated her arguments about the release date for Crystal; they had as little effect on Red as they had had on Ivor. Red also seemed to believe that Jane was persisting in error only because of slavish and inappropriate respect for Georgia. He, too, told her that the three of them, to their surprise, had come to respect her and were pleased with her efforts in managing the team. "I like it that you're here, with us, no matter how late. And I think it's great the way you went through every one of those field test reports and checked back with Arco about them. But what I can't see is this. Now you know we're not ready to roll out. So how come you won't tell Malcolm to hold off? God, it seems like the worst possible luck. We got rid of Georgia, we thought we were saved, and boom! Here you come wearing the same hat."

Jane felt a chill. "Got rid of Georgia? What do you mean?"

"Sorry, sorry, sorry," he said, running the words together as if they were one expression of regret. He leaned forward, towards her, to emphasize his apology. Jane was sitting across from his desk, which was covered with papers, magazines, computer tape cassettes, floppy disks and coffee cups. Not an inch of its surface was visible. His desk faced outwards, towards the door of his small office. Behind him, on tables, were his computers. They, too, were surrounded by open binders, books and stacks of printout paper. Now he put his elbows on top of his papers, rested his bearded chin in his hands and stared at Jane, or rather, just past her shoulder, at something in his own mind, which seemed to be resident just beyond her. "Look, I didn't mean any of us wanted something bad to happen to Georgia. But face it, she was screwing up. Okay, she did a good job as manager—paperwork, filling out forms, keeping the top brass out of our hair. But then she went off track and we couldn't get her back. For the last few months she was driving us crazy, saying we were ready to go, when we weren't. You can't blame us for being glad she's not around any more to foul things up. Is that so terrible?"

"You know I thought the world of Georgia," Jane said gently. "Naturally it sounds terrible to me, considering what happened to her."

"Okay, all right, I take it back. Have it your way. The point is—we played fair with her while she was here—we'll play fair with you. That's what I told Ivor and I'm telling you the same. But my idea of fair is that you say how you feel and then you go after what you want. No bullshit. So you've been warned, okay? The three of us will do everything . . . fair . . . to stop Crystal going out before it's ready."

Jane stood up. "I think what you're saying is you'll try to argue. But if I ever think for a moment that you're not working full out to meet the deadline, that you're doing anything to hold it back—"

"Hey! I didn't mean that! You're twisting my words around. I said fair, right? I meant trying to get you and Malcolm to see it our way. Okay?"

"No. It's not okay. I told Ivor earlier today, and I'm going to tell Catherine. I don't want to hear this matter discussed again. It's closed. You either co-operate one hundred percent or I don't want you on the team."

"Wait a minute. Whoa. Back up there. Don't get all excited. We only want what's best for Crystal, same as you." His eyes met hers for the first time. He looked sad, humbled. "You're not really mad, are you? Come on, Jane."

To Jane, Red now seemed like a dog who has just been kicked, who, instead of snarling back, becomes servile, begs for affection, tries desperately to please as long as his master is present. But dogs like that, she thought, were the very ones who jumped on your favourite chair the moment you were out of the room, and ate up the snack you had left waiting on the table. Even thinking that, she couldn't help wanting to reassure him, to comfort him, to pat his smooth, freckled bald head and tell him she'd see that everything came out just right. But she didn't. Unsmiling, she looked down at him. "I want you to support the planned release. If you do, everything will be fine. But if not, I meant what I said about your being off the team. And no more bad-mouthing Georgia. It bothers me."

He had recovered from his shock at her threat, and realized placating her with apologies was not going to work. "No one will tell you anything about Georgia you don't want to hear," his voice was spiteful. "Count on it. Will that make you happy?"

I haven't handled him well, Jane thought. Or Ivor either. I stood up to them, I held my ground, but they're just as antagonistic as ever. Why do I fly off the handle whenever anybody says anything critical of Georgia? I've really got to get hold of myself. She made up her mind to handle Catherine better. After all, woman-to-woman, that, surely, should be easier to deal with.

Of the three offices, Catherine's showed the least personality. A standard bookshelf with standard books: reference books, software documentation, textbooks, boxes of specialized journals. On her desk there was a pile of magazines with their corners strictly aligned, a mug with her name, "Catherine," and a pink rose on it and a jar of sharpened pencils. Her office was the biggest of the three, as she was nominally the most senior of the group. As a linguist, it was Catherine's work that had made possible Crystal's capacity to communicate in ordinary words, natural language. Now, making small talk to which Catherine responded unsmiling, in her flat, monotonous voice, Jane decided that Catherine was one of the few people she had met in life who owed her success and her accomplishments entirely to her intellectual ability and discipline. Most of the people whom Jane regarded as successes seemed to Jane to have accomplished what they had partly through their specific talents, and partly because of their ability to charm or inspire others. How was it possible, Jane wondered, for Catherine to conceal herself so completely?

But whatever Catherine's true nature, she wasn't going to expose it to Jane. Now she sat straight in her chair, took a pencil out of her jar, drew a pad towards her and held the pencil as if to ensure that anything agreed upon would be recorded accurately. She bent her head to look down at her pad, and Jane, seeing the neat part in Catherine's thin, sandy hair, felt Catherine's vulnerability. When Jane spoke she chose her words carefully, as if the slightest error in phrasing or choice of words might shatter Catherine's precarious façade.

"I wanted to hear from you just exactly how you feel about Crystal," Jane said, "about its going out as scheduled."

"You do?" Catherine said, looking up, surprised. She flushed suddenly, her ears and neck reddening. "You've talked to Ivor and Red, and you want to know if I back them up?"

"No, I know you back them up, Catherine. They've told me that, you've told me that. But I want to understand why."

"Why?" said Catherine, looking puzzled. "Well, I guess because their arguments make sense. Of course, there certainly was a great deal to be said for the other side, for Malcolm's view and for Georgia's. Malcolm has a sizeable amount of money tied up in Prospero and investors he has to satisfy. So it's understandable that he's in a hurry. And Georgia? Well, she took the manager's view. That's what Ivor thinks. And the facts tend to support it. She had her professional reputation tied up in coming out on time, just as we have ours in Crystal's being the best possible piece of software. It was, it seems to me, a natural tension. Maybe even . . . a creative tension."

"Do you think Ivor raised the issue of delay when I came along, because he thought, with Georgia gone, there'd be no one to uphold the other side, and he'd get his way?"

"His way?" Catherine said. She slowly put the pencil back in the jar and moved the pad over to the side of her desk. "No, I don't think so. Of course, when Ivor is convinced of something he's very determined and Red always goes along. I find it's best to let them get it out of their system. I just want to do my job. I haven't got time for a lot of this."

"A lot of what?"

"You know, personality conflicts, office politics."

"But how can you say that, Catherine? What you do counts. You can't opt out. You've supported Ivor. You could have supported Georgia, but you didn't."

"Georgia didn't need my support."

"Why do you say that?"

"Georgia was an amazing person," Catherine said slowly. "Because of her academic background, she understood my work better than anyone. We used to have long talks about linguistics, philosophy, and we did some really good work together on the user interface. The thing about Georgia was, once she decided what was right, she was just so . . . at home with it. She didn't need anyone."

"You sound like you admired her."

"Oh, I did. I know you were a friend of hers, Jane. You were very lucky. She was a wonderful person and she contributed a great deal of what is special to Crystal. She was more than just a project manager. So it was hard to understand her disagreement with Ivor. How could she turn against the project at the end, try to see it go off less than perfect?"

"I've read her project diaries," Jane said. "She didn't turn against the project. Not at all. She thought it was good enough. No piece of software is ever perfect."

Catherine smiled, her small, disconsolate smile. "That was one of her phrases. I remember her sitting right there, saying it to me when we argued about this very thing. And we agreed to disagree. I guess it's the same now. It all seemed so clear to me—that we should wait—I guess I thought Georgia wasn't acting rationally. And I had trouble with that. We drew apart; we didn't work as closely together. I felt the loss of her then, but it seems that was nothing to the way I miss her now. . . ." She paused, and Jane let the silence stretch out between them. "Jane," Catherine said, "does anybody know, have any idea, who could have . . . I mean, it must have been a stranger, a psychopath. Nobody suspects anyone close to her, do they?"

"I'm not sure," Jane said. "I guess, right now, everyone is a suspect. I know the police are still investigating—but as far as I can tell, they aren't getting anywhere."

"Well," Catherine said, "I hated to side with Ivor against her. Hated it. I wish all that had never happened. I hope they find whoever did that to her and I hope they really punish him. I miss her very, very much."

CHAPTER 22

As she drove up the gravel driveway, Jane felt an unexpected sensation of pleasurable anxiety. Malcolm's large house was lit up, the light streaming from the big casement windows in the front, out into the darkening summer night.

The house looked inviting. Jane, recognizing her longing for a time of calm, reminded herself the orderly well-kept façades of the homes of the rich were illusions. She knew—she had lived in such a house with her husband; he still lived in one. And Tom, too—his house with its masses of dried flowers, its stripped pine furniture, copper pots and plump down-filled furniture. How cosy and inviting a life it had seemed to offer. She thought of Tom. He had been away for almost two weeks and she missed him. At the same time, it was hard to deny that not having to live constantly fearing those sudden explosions of inexplicable jealous rage was restful.

She parked the car, turned off the lights, and sat for a minute hoping her inexplicable feeling of excitement would abate. She had driven up from

town with the Triumph's top off, and now, in the
silence of the summer evening, she could hear the
loud whirring sounds of the cicadas and the harsh,
insistent chirping of crickets. It calmed her. She
had brought the car to rest under a big maple; its
leaves stirred in a slight gust of wind and she heard
faintly in the distance the barking of foxes. A feeling of peace passed over her. With it came an
impulse of joy and affection, without an object.
The elongated shadows of the tree branches on
the gravel drive and the smooth lawn filled her
with pleasure. She hugged the sensations of natural beauty to herself, treasuring them, sensing that
her perceptions were heightened for some reason,
allowing her this moment.

The front screen door opened and Malcolm
came out. As she saw his long shadow advancing
towards her, her calm vanished to be replaced by
an unpleasant sensation, almost like fear. He
leaned over the car and kissed her on each cheek.
"Welcome to Maplewood Farm," he said. "Come
on in, you must be wanting a drink after battling
Friday evening traffic from town." As he helped
her step out of the car by taking her arm, she was
aware of the pleasant scent of his aftershave. She
was surprised at and alerted by the small courte-
sies, so unlike his usual behaviour when they met
on business. He's just signalling me that this is a
social occasion, not a business one, she told herself, but her feelings of anxious excitement
returned.

He led her into the living-room, which stretched
the whole length of the house. A small round table

had been set at the far end, with long screened windows open to the night. Candles burned on the table, which was set with silver and crystal.

"The bathroom is through there," he said. "Go on through; I'll pour us some drinks. What would you like?"

The candlelight, the beautifully set table, the peaceful scented evening—the atmosphere made Jane ill at ease. Having driven up from town, she also felt windblown and not sufficiently elegant for the setting. "A good Scotch," she said. "I really am very tired. It's been a rough week."

Like the rest of the house, the small powder-room was clean and ordered. Peering at her face in the mirror, Jane saw that her cheeks were flushed, her eyes bright, that she looked surprisingly good. Her hair, blown by the wind, stood out around her head in a mass of dark blonde waves. Quickly she washed her face, redid her eye-liner, but left off all the other make-up she usually wore, combed her hair flat, brushed her teeth with a little toothbrush she carried in her purse, and straightened her silk blouse. On the drive up, she had opened the second button of her blouse to enjoy the cool air; now she buttoned it up. But still, when she looked back into the mirror her face glowing with colour and life looked back at her, as if within her lived another more adventurous woman who was indifferent to Jane and unwilling to abide by her rules.

Malcolm served Jane cold soup from a large earthenware tureen, and then brought in from the kitchen a platter of pasta primavera and a big glass bowl of salad. From the faint noises in the kitchen Jane realized that he had someone staying late to cook for them, and this increased her unease. Malcolm talked to her about his farm, about his horses that he loved, and the house that he had spent ten years renovating. There was nothing personal in his conversation, nothing worrying to her in his expression or in the way he looked at her.

She could not understand what was going on. On the one hand, the dinner, the candlelight, the way he had looked down at her in the car, her own physical response. On the other, his calm, relaxed friendly manner. They talked about Pat, too.

"I guess I'm a little bitter still," Malcolm said. "I don't know how you feel about your ex-husband, but, as far as I'm concerned, a divorce is like some kind of operation. You may get well afterwards, but you always have a scar, and sometimes it aches when it rains. Do you know what I mean? Every time I think of how she left me, I have to work hard not to get mad. I would get angry, I think I have a right to, but I don't want her to have the satisfaction. And yet, I still think a lot of Pat. We had twenty good years together and that's not something you just wave goodbye to."

"It was nice of you to offer her part of the farm, the house, all that."

"It was just business. I wanted to make her a good offer when she was still feeling guilty, so she'd settle and I could get on with my life. I have a reputation for being a tough fighter; I'd get no sympathy if I went to court against a wife of twenty years who could prove I'd been seeing other women."

"Was that what it was?"

"You mean Pat's never told you? That surprises me. I loved her, but I've never been a one-woman man. Pat knew that when she married me. She put up with it for years; then, she said she couldn't take it any more. She said that getting to the top in her profession had raised her self-esteem, or something like that. I didn't understand what she was talking about. But the truth of the matter was she found someone else. And found out she liked living alone and having lovers. That's what I think. I've noticed lately quite a lot of women in their forties and fifties don't want to be married."

Jane doubted it. Didn't everyone want to be married, to be safe from loneliness, safe from the dark? It was just that the potential husbands had so many women to choose from. There were many young, compliant, beautiful, thin women willing to do anything to please, be anyone the man wanted, tell him anything. Pat was just making a virtue of necessity.

They had finished one bottle of wine and were on the second, sitting across from one another in the living-room. Malcolm brought in cognac and coffee, and Jane felt herself sliding into a relaxed euphoria. The tensions and worries of the week were washed away; Malcolm's calm manner, so different from his workaday high-voltage personality, had lulled her until her guard was down and she felt at home and comfortable. So when he made the first move, she hardly took it in.

"You really are a beautiful woman, Jane," Malcolm said, smiling at her, his tone relaxed.

"No I'm not, but it's nice of you to say so. Don't say any more about it."

"I will if I want to. And I want to."

Alarm bells now went off for Jane. She was alone in the house of a man whom she found extremely attractive. She was slightly drunk and very tired. She was lonely and he seemed to offer warmth and welcome. She wanted him; two weeks away from Tom made her particularly vulnerable. But this man was, at the moment, her boss. He might be tangled up in the death of Georgia, and most of all she loved Tom. She had been stupid, really stupid. If she turned him down, wounded his ego, he would make her pay. And she didn't want to turn him down.

Jane stood up. Malcolm stood up too. She turned to the sofa and picked up her purse. Then she walked over to him, and before he realized what she was going to do she kissed him on both cheeks, exactly as he had done when he greeted her, then pulled away. "Thank you for a wonderful evening, Malcolm. I think I'd better go right now, before I stay. I'll come back and ride tomorrow, say ten o'clock?"

She was walking towards the door, Malcolm following her. "But Jane, why not stay here? Why bother to go to Pat's and come back?"

She turned and smiled at him. "I want to stay, Malcolm. You know I do. But you and I work together. Let's not get ourselves all mixed up, okay?"

She was getting into her car, putting the key into the ignition. He leaned over it, put his hand gently on her hair. "I'm not mixed up."

"Great," she said, smiling, turning on the ignition. "But I am. We'll talk tomorrow, when I'm not so tipsy."

"Of course, Jane, if that's what you want."

He backed away from the car, putting his hands in his pockets and looking at her with a bemused, hard, slightly cynical expression. "See you tomorrow," she called out over the roar of the engine. She backed around and then took off, spurting gravel behind her on to the perfectly groomed grass, the walk, the swept flagged path, and drove away. In her rear-view mirror she saw him standing, watching her. What a God-awful idiot I am, she thought. And all the way to Pat's house her body reproached her, the lust aroused by her host, by the evening, the food and the liquor, all coursing through her system leaving her feeling quite ill.

CHAPTER 23

Jane awoke suddenly. Her heart was racing. She felt as if she were drowning; strong rhythmic waves of anxiety and nausea passed over her. Her skin was clammy. With an effort she sat up in bed and tried to orient herself. She had fallen asleep, quickly, dreamlessly, in Pat's guest bedroom. The window was wide open, and outside Jane could see the night sky, covered with faint, milky luminescent streamers of clouds. She got up, walked to the window and looked out.

Her bedroom was on the side of the house. A sweep of lawn led down to a wide belt of trees, now a blur in the cloudy night. Although the night was warm, Jane shivered. She walked back to her bed, climbed in, huddled in the centre and piled the covers over herself. But in a minute the waves of anxiety returned, stronger than ever, and she broke out in a sweat. She threw the covers off, got up and quickly, despite feeling very weak, put on a shirt and jeans, walked quietly down the hall in her bare feet, slid open the doors to the deck and went outside.

The clouds were racing across the moon, concealing it. The same wind tossed the tops of the trees. In the dark the shapes of the buildings, the side of the house, the garage, the distant roofs of Malcolm's barn, could just be seen.

Jane sat down in a deck chair and curled her feet under her. When will I learn, she thought. When will I stop making these dreadful mistakes? Why do I do it? Because I am just not a good person, that's why. And I never seem to get any better. When I was twenty-one, I let my husband take my children. I didn't try to get them back. I let him keep them and shape their lives, and lost forever the chance to be their mother when they were small. Now they've turned on me and what can I do about it? I can't make them mine, make them love me. I can't undo it. I thought because my husband had money and power he could give them security. I must have thought that meant love. And then, tonight, what did I do? I wanted Malcolm and he must have known. Why do I never learn? What's wrong with me—that I'm drawn to powerful men when I ought to have learned they bring me only unhappiness? Tonight I nearly betrayed Tom and wrecked my professional life, too, and I don't even know why.

Could I have given up my children so I would be free to go after money and power for myself because I want them so badly? At this thought, she felt such pain that she wrapped her arms around her knees and rocked back and forth in the deck chair to keep from crying out.

I'll think about something else, she thought. It's

too terrible. But then she said to herself, no you won't, Jane, you'll think about this. Surely I gave up the children because I wanted what was best for them, and because I thought I couldn't give it to them. But I was mixed up. I confused money, security and love. Now when it looks as if the kids are turning on me, I can see how wrong I was. My selfish instincts to keep them were right. But how do you know when to trust your feelings?

Tonight, every instinct seemed to be driving me into Malcolm's bed. I'll never know why I left. God, how I wanted him, still want him. And that wanting disgusts me because more than ever I want to love Tom and be loyal to him and stay with him. Oh, it's impossible! It's all such a mess.

She began to shiver. She got up, went inside, into the kitchen, poured herself a big tumbler of water, drank it down, poured herself another and took it outside. On the tiled floor, in the dim, filtered moonlight, she saw her damp footprints, the top marks like small stains.

I have to get hold of myself, Jane thought. One step at a time. I can't get away from this badness in me; I'll have to live with it and try to control the damage I do. I have to try to get the kids back, so that they know their mother really loves them. However much it hurts that I can't be the mother I long to be. And I have to say no to Malcolm so he knows I mean it. I have to find out who killed Georgia, and why, because otherwise nothing makes sense. . . .

Pat found Jane fast asleep on the deck chair when she came out on to the deck about ten the next morning, wearing a swimsuit and carrying a cup of coffee.

"Jane! I thought you were still asleep. What time did you get in last night anyway? I waited up until eleven o'clock, then gave up on you."

Jane groaned, rolled over on the deck chair, swung her legs over the side and sat up. Her body was stiff and she had the imprint of plastic cushion cover pressed into her cheek. She rubbed her eyes. "God, I'm sick. Yech. Give me a minute, Pat."

It was already very hot. Jane scratched a rash of mosquito bites on her hands and wrists and drank down the tepid water left in her glass. "If I felt any worse, I'd be dead," she grumbled. But actually it wasn't true. The emotions of the night had passed through her. She felt empty, weak and peaceful. "Hang on a sec, Pat, I'll be right back and say good morning properly." She went in, took a quick shower, put on her swimsuit, found that Pat had made coffee, helped herself and then returned to the deck.

"Oh, boy, too much booze at Malcolm's last night," she said.

"Is that all?" Pat said smiling.

"I know what you're thinking, Pat, and the answer is no. I was tempted, but I didn't sleep with him."

"You can tell me, Jane, it's nothing to me now who Malcolm sleeps with."

"Really," Jane snapped. "I wouldn't do anything to hurt Tom, and that's that."

"Okay, okay, no need to be so self-righteous. It's just that Malcolm's pretty hard to resist when he sets his mind on something. Even Georgia couldn't always stand out against him when he wanted something."

"Listen," Jane said, suddenly turning on Pat, her face flushing, "I've had it up to here with innuendoes about Georgia. From you, from everybody. I want to know what it is you're not telling me. I'm *going* to know what everyone's not telling me. All right?"

"Hey, Jane, calm down—"

"No, I won't calm down. Let's get to it. Let's start with your party. I want to hear everything Georgia did that night. There's something pretty peculiar about all the stories about the party: something people aren't telling me; something that doesn't add up."

"What are you talking about? It was just your average drunken Yuppie get-together."

"Let's start from the beginning, and remember it logically, okay? What time did Simon and Georgia get there?"

"For Christ's sake, Jane. That was weeks ago. There's too many parties in my life for me to remember details like that."

"Well, did they come together?"

Pat leaned back in her deck chair, closed her eyes and tilted her face up to the sun. Sweat glistened on her forehead and ran in rivulets down her breasts, darkening the top of her swimsuit. There was a long silence. Then Pat said in a quiet, surprised voice, "As a matter of fact, now that you lean on me, I do remember something. I remember Simon coming in, and asking for Georgia. He said that they had come in separate cars, they'd each come directly from work—you know he works in Mississauga, and she in Markham—so taking separate cars made sense. And he said he'd seen her get out of her Volvo station-wagon and walk up the drive just before him."

"And you said?"

"God knows. I probably told him what I told everyone—that she'd gone to put her raincoat in the bedroom, that he should do the same, have a drink, and so on."

"What was Georgia wearing that night, Pat?"

Pat sighed. "Honest to God, Jane. I don't know why you think I would remember that."

"Okay, let's try this. What was Ariela wearing?"

Pat was silent for a moment. Then she said in a very soft voice, "A dark green silk blouse, very tight jeans, high flat-heeled dark green leather boots, gaudy silver jewellery and a big black leather belt with silver studs. She had a lot of make-up on and looked like a tart. I realized what Malcolm had seen in her."

Jane was distracted from her line of questions. "Malcolm? Ariela?"

"Oh, Jane, be your age. Every eligible man who has met Ariela has slept with her. She's famous for her 'scrapbook.'"

"What?"

"She collects rich or famous or gifted or distinguished—or whatever—men. But the thing about Ariela is she falls in love with them first. She can fall in and out of love in about two days. She's lethal. Believe me."

"Did you see her and Simon at your party?"

"Of course I did. Everyone did. When she and Simon went outside, they were all over each other. It was impossible to miss. Ariela wanted everyone to see that if she wanted to get Simon back for a night, it was no problem. And maybe, Simon wanted people to see too. Being married to Georgia might have been a bit much for him at times. Everyone admired her so."

"Did Georgia see?"

"I'm sorry, Jane. But she must have. Those who didn't actually see them go out with their arms around each other were talking about it. It's not the kind of thing most people do, you know that. And Ariela's goings-on are pretty high profile. I'm sure Malcolm heard about it because he mentioned it to me. And I know he's been seeing her on occasion, off and on, for the last few years. So have lots of other men you know. Most of the men who were friends of Simon and Ariela when they were married were Ariela's lovers either before they divorced or after. She's a whore."

"That's not how she struck me."

"Okay, that's not the right word for her. How about promiscuous? Anyway, you know what I mean."

"What time did Georgia leave?"

"I can't remember."

"That's what's so strange, Pat. No one can remember. No one can remember what she was wearing or what time she left."

"Well, I am sure of one thing. I didn't see her after Ariela and Simon came back in. Because when I saw them come in, about half an hour after they went out, I looked for her. I wanted to lend her some moral support, you know? But she wasn't there. Someone told me she left soon after they went out. It's not hard to see why."

"Do you remember who told you that, who saw her leave?"

"No, sorry. Of course I've tried to, the police asked, but it's all an alcoholic blur."

"You know," Jane said thoughtfully, "the thing that's so surprising is that Georgia got murdered. If anyone in this bunch looked like they might arouse murderous passions, it's Ariela. Lots of people might have wanted to see the end of her, even, I suppose, Georgia. But she's still around, happy as a lark."

"Jane, I don't mean to be rude, but aren't you supposed to be over at Malcolm's today? Didn't you tell me you were coming up to go riding with him?"

"Oops," said Jane, looking at her watch. "We agreed ten-thirty, and it's that now. But one more thing before I go. You know you said I shouldn't try to find out what happened to Georgia, but when I asked you why, you refused to tell me. Now you have to. You can see that I'm not going to stop: I think you owe it to me to let me know what was behind that warning."

Pat had been leaning back, her face tilted up to the sun, her eyes closed, as she spoke. Now she twisted around, swung her legs over the side of the lounge chair and slowly sat up, facing Jane, leaning towards her as she spoke. "I know it sounds strange, Jane, but the truth is I don't know. I just feel . . . on the one hand, you are so tough and ambitious and professional, it seems you'll do anything to get where you want to go. And on the other hand, in your personal life, you seem to me to be so fragile. The way you talk about Georgia, it's as if you're just standing there waiting for someone to throw a pie in your face."

"Fine. So what's the pie? What are you worried about?"

Pat shrugged. "I'm not sure."

Jane didn't believe Pat. Her expression, her gestures, her voice, everything told Jane that Pat was lying. But it was also obvious that nothing Jane could say would make Pat change her mind. Pat believed that she was protecting her friend, and was going to go on doing so no matter what Jane said.

Jane sighed, got up, touched Pat gently on the shoulder. "I'm going now, as soon as I change. I'll be back tonight, and we can talk again. Think about it. I hope you'll see my side of it. Ignorance is not bliss; it might help me to know what I'm walking into."

Pat leaned back, tilted her head up towards the sun and closed her eyes. "I very much doubt it," she said.

CHAPTER 24

Jane found Malcolm in the paddock, inspecting two horses, both saddled and bridled. His greeting was warm; he seemed very relaxed. But his look, as he took in her windblown hair, faded jeans and scuffed riding boots, was too appreciative for a friend's. She smiled back at him, without meeting his eyes, resisting the powerful attraction she felt, realizing that the desires aroused the night before had not faded, had, if anything, grown more insistent.

Malcolm dressed in old jeans, a faded madras shirt and beautifully polished riding boots, he looked tan, fit and full of a controlled healthy energy, which Jane found exciting despite her desire not to. He handed her a hard hat, which she strapped on; it was a welcome protection against the sun, which had grown very hot.

The air was full of the scent of cut grass, of dust, of horses. From the stand of maples at the end of the paddock came the sound of crows, calling out the alarm, raucous and mocking.

The horses trotted down the lane side by side.

Malcolm told Jane that he was going to take her in a circuit around the property and then out towards the escarpment. "Are you up for a whole day? I know you don't ride regularly; you'll be stiff."

"It's okay," Jane said happily. "It will be worth it." As soon as she was on horseback, she was happy. The horse responded to every pressure of her knees and thighs; she felt the power in him as he gathered himself together and went into a canter. The white fence rails passed by in a blur, the air was soft and warm against her cheek, the rhythm of the horse almost as satisfying and sensual as sex.

Malcolm had cantered ahead of her. His horse, a big chestnut with two white stockings, had a longer, faster gait. Jane let him go. If he wanted to compete, he could do it without her. She was enjoying the sun, the heat; even the dust on her lips felt good. There was no need to rush anything, just let it go, its natural rhythm was the right one. Everything would work out if she stopped pushing so hard, stopped willing.

Ahead of her, Malcolm slowed to a trot, then a walk. She came up alongside of him. "Let's not tire the horses," he said. "It's hot, they need a breather. Where did you learn to ride?"

"I don't really know how I got interested," Jane said. "I'm a city kid. I was raised in Chicago and no one in my family knew a thing about horses. My dad was a chemist, a university professor, until he got into trouble during the McCarthy era. When I was oh, eight, nine, I started reading horse books, and got the bug. I got my mother to give me riding lessons; then, for a while, when the family ran out of money, I worked in the stables so I could keep on riding. You know those teenage girls who hang around horses? I was one of those. It lasted until I was fourteen, or fifteen, I guess, when I found out boys were better."

He laughed and Jane realized she had grown too relaxed and was in danger of repeating her mistake of the night before. He was smart enough to realize, from watching her ride the time before, that, for her, horses and sensuality were connected. It was why, she thought, he had invited her to ride in the first place.

"I'd like to talk to you about what's going on at Prospero," Jane said.

"Let's not spoil a beautiful day with business; we can talk about it later."

"No. I want to talk about it now. I need your help."

"Jane—"

"I've been trying to find out what I can about the possibility that Ivor, Red and Catherine are thinking of taking the Crystal technology to another company. I've spent a lot of time on it and I haven't heard a whisper."

"So, you think we don't have a problem there?"

"We can't be sure. I think we're going to have to act as if they're loyal. But even if they are loyal, they're not being co-operative. They're not working hard enough to meet their deadlines. I'm going to have to push them. If I push them too hard, they may leave. What do you think?"

"Can we do it without them?"

"We can do it with replacements. We'll lose credibility, but I think we'll be okay. I think it's a risk worth taking."

"What's the worst that can happen if they leave?"

She smiled. The horses were walking along a trail through some low brush. Malcolm, slightly ahead of Jane, bent a branch back so that she could pass. It sprang into place behind her with a whistling sound. "For Prospero, the worst is that we'll have a harder sell with the technical press without them. But we can handle it. Then, of course, there's the question of Georgia. Did what happened to her have anything to do with her determination to get Crystal out on time? If it did, your guess is as good as mine about what the worst is that could happen to me—if it looks like I'm going to succeed."

"You're not serious, Jane. If I thought for a moment you were in that kind of danger. . . . Do you have any reason to think so?"

"Reason? No, no reason."

They rode on in silence. "But I wouldn't feel comfortable bringing in any of the possible replacements for Georgia that I've found under these circumstances. You can understand that."

"I don't see any danger to you. I don't believe that. And I don't want a replacement—I want you."

Jane ignored the double entendre. "Okay, I'll play it as it seems best." She smiled at him thinking that now, when he was in such a good mood, might be a chance to get some of her other questions answered. "About Ariela . . ."

"What does she have to do with anything?"

"I'm not sure. What do you think of her?"

"Ariela is a very attractive woman. Very beautiful."

"What did she think of Georgia? She said she loved Georgia—do you think that's true?"

"Oh, Ariela worshipped Georgia. She wanted to have the same ability to control herself, to control things, that Georgia had. Ariela is an idealist; she sees the best in everybody and envies them."

"Yes," Jane said, "they're certainly very different. Hard to believe they were married to the same man—most people are attracted to the same type over and over."

"Well, those two certainly aren't the same type. Ariela is all emotions, not that she isn't bright, but she doesn't really think seriously about anything. Now Georgia, she was a thinking person who could get things done. She had great presence. Georgia wasn't beautiful, but if she were in the same room with Ariela, once she started to speak, you wouldn't even notice Ariela."

"Malcolm, Pat said you had an affair with Ariela."

"One thing about Pat, she never minds talking about things which are none of her business."

"Did you?"

"I don't see that it's your business either."

"Ariela wouldn't care if you told me, you know that. I'll ask her, and she'll tell me."

"It didn't mean anything. It was just one of those things that happens—for a week or two you're wildly infatuated; then, you can't think what got into you."

"And Georgia? Did you sleep with her too?"

He was astounded. Their horses both stopped, cued by their riders' unconscious signals. "Georgia? Jane, what are you thinking about? Let's sit down, it's almost noon. We'll have lunch and get to the bottom of this."

They had ridden off the trail, along the road, and were now passing through rolling land, covered here and there with small copses of trees. They rode into one, found a level shady patch and tethered the horses. Malcolm had brought a blanket and a light lunch. He must have always been intending to stop at the spot he had chosen, because there was a small stream with a pebbly bottom for the horses to drink from and in which he could chill the wine. He unwrapped sandwiches, cold chicken, fruit, slices of cake.

"Now, about Georgia," he said. Jane could see that the question had offended him. He was no longer flirting. He was annoyed. On guard. "Let me put it to you this way—I respected Georgia; she was a colleague. Georgia and I were working together on something that could be a very major deal for me—if it succeeds—and a bloody expensive disaster if it fails. That's how I thought of Georgia. The only way I thought of her."

Jane wondered why Malcolm found the idea of his sleeping with Georgia so offensive. Perhaps it was because she was ugly, or maybe he thought of Georgia as an equal and thus not suitable for seduction. If the latter, his behaviour towards Jane could be seen more as an insult than a compliment. But Jane wondered if he was covering up something. Otherwise, why would he react so strongly to the suggestion that he and Georgia had been lovers? Maybe there was something else? She decided to see if she could bluff him.

"But I thought you and Georgia disagreed? Originally you tried to postpone Crystal, because Ivor, Red and Catherine convinced you it wasn't ready. But she had the rest of Prospero behind the idea of immediate release. With the power of her personality, once she was opposed to delay, you had a problem. Had Georgia become a real obstacle to you?"

"I don't appreciate this, Jane. I don't like what you are implying. Of course Georgia and I had our disagreements. Perhaps I did tend towards delay, at one time. But at the end I saw we had to do it Georgia's way. I came to the realization the woman had more courage than any of us. And I backed her one hundred percent."

He glared at Jane. Whatever attraction had been between them was gone. Jane had challenged him on his turf, and he didn't like it. He was angry with her, looking at her with dislike. And Jane, once he no longer admired and wanted her, found that she no longer wanted him. For a moment she was tempted to smile, to flirt, to placate him. She resisted the temptation. "And Simon, where does he come in?"

Malcolm took a sandwich out of its wrapping and bit into it. "Simon is a lightweight. Georgia was too good for him. It's hard to believe he could hurt a woman like Georgia, for Ariela. It would be like going to McDonald's when you have a live-in four-star chef."

"Come on, Malcolm," Jane said, irritated. "You've already said you cheated on Pat. Isn't it the same thing?"

"No, it's not. You don't understand. You don't do something like that in front of your wife unless you want to hurt or humiliate her. If you love your wife, you protect her; the things you do never touch her."

"Sometimes I think I'll never understand men, never." She sighed, stretched out on the blanket, a plastic glass of wine balanced in her hand. It was very peaceful. Occasionally a seed pod fell from the tree on to the blanket, a wasp lumbered over the slices of cake. Beyond the trees, the horses cropped at the grass; Jane could hear the sound as they ripped the grass up and munched at it.

"You're kind of hard to understand yourself, Jane. What about you, are you faithful to Tom?"

"Yes."

"And if he were unfaithful to you?"

She sat up and refilled her wineglass. "I don't know. I haven't thought about it." I have too much to contend with, with his jealousy, to have any of my own, she thought. But the truth was she found it impossible to imagine Tom unfaithful. He was such a good lover, so interested in her, so willing to do everything and anything to please her. She couldn't conceive of him with another woman.

"I should warn you, Malcolm. I'm going to find out who killed Georgia. It's possible what I find out may disrupt Prospero. But I'm going to let the chips fall where they may."

"Just a minute. What do you mean?"

"I mean just what I said."

"No, I'm sorry, Jane. I can't allow that. I don't want anything to interfere with the launch of Crystal. There's millions riding on it—I have a lot of investors. Frankly, I can't afford it."

"That's too bad."

"Did you hear what I said? I told you to lay off."

Jane could see that he was having trouble believing her, having trouble believing that this small blonde woman, whom he had thought suitable as an employee, as a stooge, as a chess-piece on his chess-board, as a pleasurable sexual challenge and conquest, was going to thwart him in business. This was a side of him she had not seen and she didn't like it. His face was darkening with anger, his thick eyebrows drawn together, his mouth narrow and tight. Jane felt afraid.

"I said you'll do nothing until Prospero is launched. You are working for me. And that's the way it's going to be. Do you understand?"

Jane got up, wrapped her uneaten sandwiches back in plastic, tucked her share of the food into the saddle-bag. She saddled her horse, packed away the halter and, with difficulty, mounted up. Malcolm was still sitting on the blanket, now looking up at her, his face suffused with anger. He didn't move to give her a leg up. "Where the hell do you think you are going? I want an answer."

"I think this meeting is over," Jane said. "I'm sorry, but it seems we must agree to disagree." She kept her voice calm, with an effort. It was difficult, even looking down at him from horseback, not to quail at the expression on his face and at the knowledge of the harm an angry and hostile Malcolm Morton could do to her. She managed a smile. "Don't worry, I won't do anything without talking to you about it first. I'll look after Prospero as best I can. But finding out what happened to Georgia comes first."

He was slightly calmer now, but still very angry. "I don't appreciate this, Jane. I won't forget it." But Jane was now beyond the point where she could be bullied by anyone, even Malcolm Morton. So she just nodded her head at him, leaving him to think, if he wanted to, that she was yielding to his pressure. Then she sat deep into the saddle, signalled the horse for a canter and took off back towards the house.

By the time she heard hoofbeats behind her, she was too far ahead for him to catch up.

CHAPTER 25

Jane had told Tom that she would be back from her country weekend on Sunday night. She had not told him that she planned to spend Friday evening having dinner with Malcolm, or that she would be riding with him on Saturday and Sunday. She had not wanted to face either a jealous outburst or the silent rage with which Tom greeted situations that made him jealous. Tom had told her that he would be back from his trip Sunday night, and she had agreed to meet him at his house then. Now, thinking that he might return early Sunday, she decided to go straight to his place. She had had enough of Malcolm and Pat. She was frightened by Malcolm's reactions, still feeling the after-effects of her night-time anxiety attack and the insights that had accompanied it, and worried by her talk with Pat. So she stopped at Pat's just long enough to pick up her things and say goodbye, and was back in town by early Saturday evening.

Not feeling like cooking, she stopped to buy some fruit and cheese. By the time she arrived at Tom's house on MacPherson Avenue, the sun was low in the sky. It had clouded over, but from time to time the sun broke through the clouds, sending out long golden rays to pick out a mass of glossy leaves on the trees that lined the street, or a brass number plate, or to shine into a house window lighting up what appeared to be a cosy *mise en scène.* Jane was happy to be back.

She parked the car in the back lane, leaving her luggage, and was glad to see Tom's car. Coming into the house the back way, she called out, "Hey, Tom, hello, I'm home." Then she noticed that in the kitchen there were two glasses of wine, half-drunk, and that one had lipstick on it. The scent of perfume was in the air. Her mind was strangely frozen as she took this in and her heart began to bang loudly in her chest. In her mind's ear she heard Pat saying, "You're just standing there waiting for someone to throw a pie in your face."

She stood in the kitchen not knowing what to do. Not wanting to go into the dining-room, the living-room, or up the stairs—afraid of what she might see. She found she was unable to call out. She heard the familiar squeak of the bedroom door opening, then the sound of someone running down the stairs and the front door banging shut.

Slowly she walked up the stairs. Tom was sitting on the bed. He was wearing only cotton trousers; his chest was bare. His clothes, including his underpants, were strewn around the room. The bed was rumpled, and the same perfume that Jane had smelt in the kitchen filled the air. Tom's elbows were on his knees, his head in his hands.

She stood at the doorway of the bedroom taking it all in, her heart pounding, her body very cold.

He looked up at her, his face expressionless, and when he spoke his voice was annoyed, slightly peevish. "You said you weren't coming home until Sunday."

Jane sat down on the bed. She wanted to run out, to leave, but her legs were too weak to carry her. Besides, it was to Tom that she wanted to run for comfort. For the past six months he had been her comforter when horrible things happened to her. "I'm sorry," she said.

"It wasn't anything, really, Jane, it was nothing. I never expected you—"

"Oh, don't say anything more. I've spent the weekend listening to lies. I can't take it any more!"

"Please don't scream at me, Jane. Let's talk about this rationally."

"Let's not," Jane said. "Now I understand. I understand why you were so jealous. You've been cheating on me, so you thought I was cheating on you. It's so obvious. How could I have missed it?"

"Were you?" he said anxiously, turning to her, biting his lip.

"No." She got up unsteadily, walked into the bathroom and leaned over the toilet. But nothing came up, although waves of nausea passed through her. Now I know what Pat was warning me about, she thought. She must have known Tom was unfaithful; probably everybody knew. They've all been laughing at me behind my back. Malcolm certainly knew. Tom probably slept with Ariela. Pat knew. Georgia knew. God, maybe that was Ariela going out the door. She sat down on the edge of the bathtub and rested her head on the sink. Why? If she knew anything, she knew Tom loved her. She knew it completely. Why had he done this? If anything, he loved her more, much more than she was capable of loving him. She was his best friend, the only person he could talk to about his feelings. Could it be that he felt trapped by his love? Felt unsafe because she couldn't love him back in the same way? That this was his escape hatch? She couldn't understand, couldn't begin to understand.

He came and stood at the bathroom door, leaning up against it. "Don't leave me, Jane."

"Aren't you even going to say you're sorry?"

He was silent.

"Aren't you even going to say it won't happen again?"

"I can't say that. I want it to be true, but probably, it's not. You know I love you with all my heart."

"Who was it? Anybody I know?"

"No, never. Nobody you know. And this is the first time I've ever brought anyone here. It's just . . . she's married, and I usually go over to her house when he's away, but tonight . . ."

The word "usually" made Jane's heart hurt. She felt a pain there, as if someone was squeezing it. She remembered the evenings she had called Tom and he had been out for half an hour, an hour. I went to get milk, he had said, or a newspaper, or to pick up the dry-cleaning. Always a gratuitous excuse. It had bothered her that he went to the trouble of explaining these absences. Why hadn't she understood? Wilfully standing there, waiting for the pie to land on her face?

"I can't be as good as you are, Jane. I try, I try hard, but it's not in my nature. I love that side of you, I don't want to lose it."

"Good?" cried Jane, losing control of herself. "Good? You poor self-deceived schmuck! Oh, it's beyond bearing that you do this to escape from me being good, that you love me because I am good!"

She brushed past him, ran down the stairs and out of the house. Her hands were shaking so much that she could barely get the car key into the ignition. Backing out, she killed the engine twice before she switched into automatic pilot and found the car moving along, as if of its own volition, along Rosedale parkway. Good? She thought to herself, the son of a bitch. The only good person that I ever knew was Georgia and look what happened to her.

CHAPTER 26

Jane was in her kitchen stirring brownies. It was Sunday, the day after her flight from Tom's house. She had not wanted to call anyone, to talk to anyone about what had happened. When her telephone rang, she let the answering machine handle it. Tom had called several times, Malcolm once. She did not want to speak with either of them. Tom sounded angry, as if, somehow, what had happened was her fault. Malcolm had sounded placatory, as if he believed that she needed to be cajoled.

Jane had spent the morning in bed. She had made herself a big pot of herbal tea, gathered the Saturday *Globe and Mail* and a pile of magazines around her, cuddled herself in a ball, drank the tea, wept and read her magazines. Around noon she felt a sudden craving for chocolate, and the idea came to her to make brownies, brownies like her mother had made for her and her younger sisters when they were children. She had gone around to the convenience store, bought the ingredients, and now the smell of chocolate and melted butter was filling the kitchen. She could not remember when she had last baked anything. Perhaps when her children had been there to visit. Five, six years ago?

I won't die of it, of the hurt, of the humiliation, she told herself as she stirred the chocolate—it's a cliché. I just have to decide if I still want him, if he still wants me, what we're going to do. In the range of hurts, it's below losing the children, it's below Bernie leaving me, even though I didn't love him anymore. If only my heart would stop aching. It's as if, physically, something happened to it when I saw those glasses on the table. As if a giant hand had reached into my chest and wrenched at my heart. Her rib-cage felt bruised, there was an actual physical ache.

Her thoughts, which had circled wildly, replaying scenes and incidents, understanding them anew, understanding so much about Tom's behaviour that she hadn't understood before, and at the same time not understanding as much as she had once thought she understood, were now circling around the puzzle of Georgia, trying to see how the two fit together. Trying to understand how Pat's fears related to what she had just learned. It must have been the party, she thought. Pat didn't want me asking questions about the party because Tom was there, because he left early, perhaps with a woman. Yes, that would explain Tom's manner when he talked about the party. Jane remembered, with great clarity, the way Tom looked at her when, telling her he had been at the party, he had said, "I thought Pat would have told

you." Certain expressions of his, certain actions
that she now understood, came back to her so
clearly. At the time they had had a peculiar reso-
nance she hadn't understood. But she had certainly never, never suspected he was deceiving her
with other women. Perhaps because she had not
been unfaithful herself, the possibility of his being
so had never been real to her.

By noon, as she stood over her stove, stirring the
chocolate, she had reached a kind of numbness.

I don't really know Tom, she thought. I made a
mistake. I believed love was a combination of
friendship and sexual attraction, sexual compati-
bility. That's what we had, still have. But there has
to be something else, something like what I felt for
Tom when I wouldn't let myself drift into bed with
Malcolm. Something maybe men don't have. She
remembered her friend Kersti telling her men
were born to hurt women, women to hurt men.
Trapped into needing each other, trapped into
wounding one another. It was true. If Tom had
realized how she had flirted with Malcolm, wanted
him, he would have felt hurt and betrayed. Silly as
that seemed to Jane, when nothing had happened,
nothing had even been said that could be considered disloyal.

As she stirred the chocolate and inhaled its fra-
grance, she stretched out her hand to the wall
phone and called Simon. Maybe Simon's charm
will help, she thought. And she could do something for Simon. He needed her. She could talk to
Simon about Georgia. That, too, would be comforting.

Simon sounded glad to hear from her. "How would you like to come over?" she asked him. "I'm making brownies."

"I'd love to. Have you had lunch yet?"

"No."

"Then how about I bring something. You can tell me what you've found out about Georgia, we'll eat my lunch and your brownies."

He brought pasta salad and bread, and they ate at the kitchen table. Simon ate two brownies politely. Jane ate half the pan. She found herself talking to Simon about Tom, not telling him what had happened, but letting out a little of the hurt.

"I'm eating all these brownies because Tom and I had a terrible fight last night. Maybe we broke up."

"What happened? Or don't you want to talk about it?"

"Just be sympathetic. It was all his fault, of course."

"Of course. It's always the man's fault. That's the worst thing about women, the thing we can't stand." He smiled as he spoke, but Jane sensed the sadness underneath.

"You and Georgia," she said hesitantly, "did you fight?"

His smile faded. "Georgia didn't fight. She didn't need to. She was usually right. But she'd give in if she saw that something meant a lot to me."

"Did you fight with Ariela?"

"Who told you about Ariela?"

"Why, is it a secret? You can hardly expect to

keep a marriage a secret."

He looked down at his hands. "That was a mistake. Something I'll regret to my dying day. Marrying her. Getting tangled up with her."

"What do you mean, tangled up?"

"Ariela left me, you know. Once she was gone, I was glad. In my position, there's a kind of life you have to lead and she didn't belong in it. We both realized we'd made a mistake. She was just too young and too . . . counter-culture, you know? But she loved me. It's confusing when someone goes on loving you and you don't love them."

"I gather she loved a lot of men," Jane said drily. She collected the dishes and stacked them in the sink. Simon helped her. They went into the living-room. Simon stretched out on the sofa, draping his feet over the arm. "Let's not talk about her, that's all over. Tell me what you've found out about Georgia."

Simon's voice sounded strained, unnatural. She wondered if her own hurt was making her over-sensitive, causing her to imagine things, to suspect things that weren't true. Suddenly she felt frightened, restless. "Let's go for a walk. We can talk outside. It's a nice afternoon. I went riding yesterday and I'm stiff; I'd like to walk it out."

They agreed to walk back to Simon's house. He lived about a mile from Jane and had walked over. They followed the winding roads, talking slowly with long pauses. Jane described the in-fighting at Prospero, telling Simon that she was worried about what Ivor was up to. She also told him about her suspicions that there had been trouble between Georgia and Malcolm over the Prospero release date. Simon didn't seem very surprised by any of it.

"Sure, Malcolm and Georgia disagreed from time to time, but they still worked well together; I think you should ignore that. But remember, I did warn you about Ivor. I'd suspect him more if he hadn't left the party with me. I just don't see how he could do it. But if you could get around that—"

"What about when you were looking for Georgia the next morning? What if she came in early in the morning, found Ivor there, and he—"

"It's just possible, Jane, but I don't believe it. And do you know why? I don't believe Georgia would stay out all night.'

"Even if she saw you and Ariela?"

They were walking down Simon's driveway. Jane turned to look at him as she spoke. He blushed, or at least his neck and ears got red. "That was the stupidest thing I ever did in my life. I'm sorry you had to find out about it." They went around to the back of the house and sat down in the garden chairs.

"Simon," Jane said, "what was Georgia wearing the night she disappeared?"

"What was she wearing?" Jane waited. "Wearing?" Simon repeated. "Uh, I think she was wearing a white silk dress, with blue trim, blue shoes. That's what she had on when they found her."

"Was it pretty, a striking dress? Like most of Georgia's clothes?"

"What kind of question is that, Jane? What are

you getting at? I mean, what does it matter?" He got up, seeming very agitated, and walked back and forth across the patio. "How would you like a drink?" When she didn't answer, he said, "Yes, it was a striking dress, a very striking dress. Maybe just what you wear to attract a murderer. How should I know?

"I want a drink. I'll get you a Scotch." He walked rapidly into the kitchen, distressed, as if the memory of Georgia and her white dress brought everything back to him.

Jane got up quickly and went into the garage. There was Simon's car, the blue BMW. There was Georgia's car, a Volvo station-wagon. Jane peered inside. She opened the door and looked in the front seat, the back seat. What was she expecting to find? Of course, the police would have examined the car much more thoroughly than she ever could. She shut the door and looked around the garage. There were skis and ski boots and poles in long racks. There were two racing bicycles, expensive, elegant ones, the woman's neglected, the man's shiny and in good repair, hanging on brackets. There were bicycle pumps, cycling helmets and goggles, repair kits, tool kits, snow-shovels, a snow-blower, an electric lawn-mower, well tended and clean. There were bags of lime and fertilizer and racks of garden tools. There were gumboots and muddy tennis shoes and stacks of grimy gardening gloves. Jane took one last look at Georgia's car. Then she went out, into the garden. Simon was coming out of the house with a tray of drinks and potato chips.

"I'm sorry," Jane said, speaking to him with difficulty. "Suddenly I don't feel very well. It's all too much . . . I'm going home. I'm sorry."

"Jane! You don't look well, you're pale. I think you should sit down."

"No, I'm going home. Right now. I've had too many shocks in the last few days; all of a sudden it's catching up to me." She turned and almost ran down the drive, out to the street.

Simon did not come after her.

CHAPTER 27

Barrodale agreed with Jane. "Yes, that's right, as far as I can tell, the only person who clearly remembers seeing Georgia at the party was her husband, who said he saw her going into the house just before him. But many of the people at the party referred to her presence; they just don't remember exactly. That's not surprising, you know."

They were sitting in the coffee room of the Serious Crimes Division on Yonge Street. Around them, plainclothesmen came and went, getting coffee in mugs or paper cups, joking, laughing. The table, Jane noticed, was scarred with long thin scratches, like shallow knife cuts.

"Well, I think it's surprising," Jane said. "No one remembered what she was wearing. That's what's so odd. No one remembers any specific conversation. And, if you knew Georgia, you'd realize how unlikely that is. You wouldn't spend ten minutes— or even five minutes—chatting with Georgia and not remember."

"Where are you going with this?"

"If no one remembers what Georgia was wearing,

or what she said or did, maybe she wasn't there at all."

"I don't get it, Jane. Even if her husband lied about seeing her going in—and sure, that's possible—how come everybody we talk to remembers that she was there?"

"I can see how unlikely it sounds," Jane said unhappily. "But suppose Simon created the idea of her being there. You know, when he met people they'd ask after her, of course. And he'd say: Oh, Georgia's in the kitchen, complaining about the food. And then they'd have a faint memory of Georgia at the party, complaining about the food. Of course, when you pressed them, they couldn't describe her because they hadn't seen her. But I know I sometimes have mental images of things people have told me that are as strong as if I'd seen them myself. Eventually, if enough time passes, I may even think I've seen them myself. So maybe Simon talked about Georgia to everyone, as if she were there, and fooled everyone into thinking she was there. Anyway, that's the only thing that makes any sense to me."

She told Barrodale about Simon and Ariela, and about Simon's throwing up. "I can't believe that Simon, no matter how much he'd had to drink, would act like that if Georgia was there. He's too sensitive a person to hurt her like that, to humiliate her, in front of her friends. And the throwing-up part—ever since I've heard that I've wondered if Simon wasn't upset about more than a sexual indiscretion."

"Wait a minute. If he pretended she was there,

chances are he killed her. Are you saying he was
the kind of guy who could kill his wife, but not the
kind of guy who could shame her in front of her
friends?"

"Oh God . . . I don't want to believe it." She put
her face in her hands, pressing her eyes shut,
pressing her fingers against her forehead, as if to
push these dreadful thoughts out of her mind.
There was a long silence. Barrodale waited
patiently. When she spoke, her voice, muffled by
her hands, was very soft, almost inaudible. "I just
can't imagine Simon hurting Georgia. But maybe,
in a fit of rage, about something, God knows what.
. . . Oh, I know, it seems impossible. But motive,
you don't need to understand motive to believe
that someone is a murderer, surely?" She took her
hands away from her face and looked up at him,
hoping—though she didn't expect it—that he
would tell her that she was wrong, that what she
was saying was impossible.

"You're right about motive. If you'd heard half
the reasons I've heard for killing someone. . . ."

"Anyway," Jane burst out, "if he did do it . . . for
whatever reasons, how could we ever understand?
To kill someone really bad, to kill someone who
stands in your way, I can kind of understand, but
this? Even though I know him well, what possible
reason could there be? How will I ever figure it
out?"

"We'll have to try, Jane. If we're going to have to
talk to everyone who was at that party to verify
your idea of Georgia's not being there, we need a
convincing theory. Motive would help. The officer

in charge of this case, he's going to be skeptical. Right now, we don't figure the husband for it. He had nothing to gain, everything to lose. But wait a minute, you say he was having an affair with his ex-wife? We never got a whisper of that."

"Not an affair. I think he saw her once in a while. Who knows, maybe being married to Georgia was kind of wearing. And men find Ariela very seductive. She knows how to love without wanting much from them, without expecting much in return except sex."

"So how do you see it? Do you think the husband killed her during a fight—maybe when she found out about this thing with the ex?"

"A fight? A fight with Georgia? No, I think Georgia would have been hurt if she'd found out, but Georgia would have understood." For a painful minute, Jane thought about herself and Tom. She supposed she would have to make the effort to try to understand. Why would a man who loved her, and she was sure of that, who, in fact, loved her more than she loved him, needed her more, betray her so casually? Destroy a relationship the two of them had tried so hard to make work? It was incomprehensible. Surely he knew—she'd told him—she needed complete fidelity in a lover to trust. And she needed trust to love. He wrecked it all for no reason that she could understand. But Simon and Georgia were different. Georgia wasn't Jane. She was a strong, powerful, confident woman who controlled her life and dominated everyone around her with the strength of her character, who would go on loving Simon

no matter what he did, who was his mate for life.
Georgia had told Jane that, though she didn't
need to—Jane had seen it. And Simon had told
her, had told her that, with his love, respect and
admiration for Georgia perfectly clear. Jane was
sure she wasn't wrong about Simon and Georgia's
relationship. How could all the practical hard facts
point one way and the emotional facts point the
other way? They only came together . . . they only
came together. . . .

"What is it, Jane, what's the matter? Are you
okay?"

"Not really," she said, her voice sounded strange,
her mouth was suddenly very dry. "I just had an
idea that's made me dizzy. Could I have a drink of
water?"

"Of course." he got up, filled a paper cup with
water and gave it to Jane. She raised her head and
drank. Her mouth was so dry she had difficulty
swallowing; the flat tepid water felt good. She
drank it down in one draught; he brought her
another and she drank that too. "These people are
my friends," she said. "My friends. Oh God."

"Tell me."

"I can't."

"If he did it, he killed your friend. Why would
you want to protect him?"

Jane looked up at the tone in Barrodale's voice.
It was the first time she had seen or heard any
emotion in him. "With what I've told you about
Ariela—that should be enough for you to check
into the facts. If anyone really remembered seeing
Georgia at the party, we can forget how I feel, what

I think, what I say or don't say."

"We'll check into it. You can count on that. And I appreciate your telling me what you found out about the ex-wife. A lot of these rich people screw around though. It's always a bit of a job to prove in court that it makes much difference. You open up that can of worms and you find out that they were all doing it to each other. Now if Georgia was fooling around, we'd have a motive."

"No."

"Okay, okay, I was just saying *if* she was. It's an old story. But it's hard to put together a guy killing his wife because she found out about the other woman. A divorce wouldn't hurt him; in his business they're a dime a dozen."

"It's so hard to understand; I know it."

"It's certainly worth checking into. We'll get people on this and I'll get back to you. If it looks like there's anything to this angle, we'll have to start checking everybody's alibi for the day of the party, at least. And that's going to be hard after all this time. We're going to have to figure out how the husband got her car and her body forty miles out of town and then got himself back. I know from checking the alibis that his car was parked in his driveway all the day before. He takes the subway to work. So if he did it, I sure don't see how."

Jane had a lunch meeting scheduled with Ivor, Red and Catherine. It was the last thing she felt like doing, but the situation at Crystal was such that she didn't want to cancel. When she walked into the restaurant and saw the three of them, Ivor looking arrogant, Red with his weak, false smile and Catherine, withdrawn and passive, Jane realized that her patience had run out.

Watch out, she told herself, don't go too fast, don't let everything else that's going on get to you—don't blow it. Heeding her own warning, she greeted them all in a friendly manner and made pleasant small talk, while they ordered their pizza and argued over the relative merits of anchovies versus pineapple.

But as soon as the waiter had taken their order, Jane gathered their attention with a look. "I wanted to have lunch with you all today because I've been thinking about our talks last week and I want to tell you what I've decided."

"You've changed your mind about the release date," Ivor said, smiling, his voice showing warmth towards Jane for the first time. "That's great!"

"No," Jane said. "Just the opposite. I've talked to marketing and I'm convinced we have no choice. We have to stick to Georgia's schedule and we will. Now listen—" she realized her anger, which perhaps had nothing to do with them, was showing in her voice and then she realized that she didn't care. "I've tried explaining to you three, but unfortunately for Prospero you only see one side—your side. I understand your side, but you don't consider anyone else's. Well I've thought about that, and I've decided it's not acceptable. Either you three get whole-heartedly behind the release or you're out of Crystal."

There was a shocked silence. "You can't do

that," Ivor said, leaning forward and glaring at her. "Only Malcolm can do that."

"I have his support," Jane lied, looking right back at Ivor. Jane thought she probably could have gotten Malcolm's support, but with the confusing cross currents in their relationship at the moment, she hadn't felt like asking him for any favours.

"Well . . . to hell with that!" Ivor said, losing his composure. "We've got share options."

"Fine. You've got share options. So what. I'm not even suggesting you'll be fired—just taken off the project and replaced by programmers who will help."

"That's ridiculous," Ivor said. "It would take new programmers months to get up to speed on our code—if they could."

"They'll have months," Jane said. "We won't need technical input until after release anyway. You've trained all the dealers' support people. Terry and Larry can handle the bits and pieces."

"Terry and Larry!" said Ivor in disgust, revealing his disdain for his junior team members.

"I intend to do this if you force it," Jane said, "so make up your mind whether you're in—on my terms—or out. That's the only choice you have."

The three of them looked at one another.

"I want to be a part of Crystal, I want to help in its release," Catherine said. "I put my heart in it, I'm not going to walk away now. I'll do what you want."

"Catherine!" Ivor said.

Jane smiled at Catherine.

"And here's another thing. I know Ivor was in my office reading files that were none of his business."

"Hey! I—" Ivor began.

"That's given rise to some ugly suspicions. Suspicions about the possibility of information being passed along to competitors, about people not being loyal to Prospero—"

"Wait a minute! I—"

She overrode Ivor's shocked protests. "I don't want to hear any explanations. Words won't resolve this. I've prepared a non-competition agreement. It obliges all of you to stay with Crystal, make your best efforts to ensure its success, keep all our trade secrets confidential, and not go into competition with Crystal for two years after you leave Prospero. You'll all have to sign this to stay at Prospero. Here, have a look." She passed around copies of a document she had prepared.

"I can't believe this!" Red said furiously. "When we've busted our asses for you." The three of them leafed through the agreement. Ivor and Red were obviously outraged, Catherine thoughtful.

"This is standard industry practice," Jane said. "I don't understand how it was missed out when you three were hired. Not having such an agreement has left you vulnerable to the kind of suspicions I've just mentioned. In any case, this isn't negotiable. You sign this or you're out."

Catherine looked up from the agreement. Her calm grey eyes met Jane's. "Everything Jane says makes perfect sense to me. There's nothing in this that doesn't accord with my intentions. I have no problem with signing this agreement. I have no problem with anything Jane is saying."

"I don't believe this," Red said. "Ivor, do we have to put up with this shit?"

"Yes, you do," Jane said. Ivor was silent, looking down at his agreement. "She's right about one thing," he mumbled without looking up, "this is a pretty standard agreement. It's fair." He raised his eyes to Jane. "I would never sell out Prospero," he said. "I can see why you doubt me, but I wouldn't. If this is what it takes to get things back on track. . . ."

They're going to swallow it, Jane thought. Catherine had broken ranks; Ivor was off balance. His position was weak because he looked so bad, having taken papers from her desk. He must realize he would have to demonstrate he could be trusted. Now it was just a question of letting him save face.

"The problems you're concerned about, Ivor," Jane said, her voice gentler, "I know they're real. I want you to start working on the next release right now. I'm hoping to move it forward. Nine months instead of a year. You've got enough improvements planned to make that possible."

"Yes, yes, that's true." He turned to look at his colleagues. Catherine returned his look without warmth. Red avoided his eyes.

"Red," Jane said, "do I have your support?"

"I have to think about it. God, it's a shitty choice."

The pizza came and they all gratefully changed the subject. But as the last piece was eaten, Jane again forced the issue. "Well? Red? Ivor? Are you in or out?" She saw Ivor look at Red, realizing, as Jane already had, that Red would side with Jane and Catherine.

"I'll call you," Ivor said.

Jane knew Ivor was going to try to change their minds. But for once she wasn't worried. At least, when it came to Crystal, things were now on track.

Red started to speak, but Ivor overrode him. "We need to think about it," he said, quelling Red with a look. "Give us a little time. If we agree, we'll want to do it one hundred percent."

"Sure, take your time, take all day," Jane said.

She put down money to pay for the lunch, pushed her chair back and got up. She had much more serious matters on her mind; this was one she was not going to let get away. "Think all you want," she said. "But call me tonight at home. Or starting tomorrow, we go on without you."

CHAPTER 28

Jane was missing Tom. The hurt he had caused her drew her towards him; she needed comforting, and Tom, the man who loved her, was the source of comfort she looked to. Perhaps if her best friend, Kersti, had not been away on assignment, Jane would have turned to her. But she was not sure; dear as Kersti was to her, close as they were, perhaps she would not have wanted Kersti to know of her humiliation. Nor would she have wanted to hear Kersti's cynical response, the negative remarks she would have made. Jane could imagine what Kersti would say. She did not think she could bear to hear all those "All men do it, what did you expect," and "Men aren't capable of love as we women mean it," etcetera. For sure she didn't want to call long-distance to Lebanon and discuss such things over the telephone. Also, she had treasured Kersti's compliments about Tom. Kersti had said he was an unusually sensitive and understanding man. Knowing the casual and thoughtless way he had betrayed Jane would probably turn Kersti against him. Jane didn't want that.

235

So that, finally, Monday evening, after her talk with Sgt Barrodale, when Tom called her, she switched off the answering machine and spoke to him, telling him yes, they should talk and yes, he could come over. Because, despite what had happened between them, she still wanted Tom's advice about what to do about Simon. She wanted to hear his insights; she thought maybe he would understand things she had failed to grasp.

Tom was looking haggard. His skin colour was poor; his clothes hung loosely as if he had shrunk inside them. Jane was glad to see it. She hoped he was suffering as much as she was. She felt a fierce delight in his misery, but this satisfaction did nothing to assuage her own pain or feelings of shame. She listened as Tom explained, again, how little his casual liaisons had meant to him. "It's just not the same thing as with you. It's just a quick thrill; it's something men do."

"I think that's disgusting," Jane said. "I'm sorry, but to me it's simple. You knew if I found out it would hurt me, and for something you say is trivial, you took that risk. It doesn't make sense. It just doesn't."

"You're right. I guess I don't understand it myself. But God, I'm sorry, Jane."

They were sitting on the sofa. He put his arms around her drawing her close. She was tense, rigid in his arms, resisting the comfort she longed for. Then suddenly a vicious torrent of sexual desire swept over her. She had never felt anything like it. He responded and they made love, quickly and violently, on the narrow sofa, Jane on top. Her pleasure was intense and fierce. There was no love or affection in it. And afterwards, she felt wonderful, while Tom looked pole-axed. She got up, put her clothes back on and sat facing him in the rocking-chair.

"Well, now that I got what I want," she said, "let's talk."

He was looking down, carefully buttoning up his shirt. When she spoke, he looked up at her. She could see that her tone and words had angered him and was astounded to realize that she did not care. His capacity for rage no longer frightened her. I believed he was angry at me, he thought he was angry at me, but really, he was angry at himself, she thought. Unless I am as close and as loving as I was before, his rage can't hurt me. And no way am I going to let myself be that close to him unless he changes. How can he change when he doesn't know why he does what he does? Her disdain felt good; for the moment, it anaesthetized her. For the moment she could believe that she was too disgusted with him to be hurt by him.

She told Tom about Simon, about her idea that Georgia had never been to the party, about her fear that Simon had lied because Georgia was already dead. "He was giving himself an alibi," Jane said. "It explains so much. He reported Georgia missing after the party, during a period when he was with Ivor and then with their friends. It was a fluke that her body was discovered. Still the delay confused the time of death. And unless the police have a believable motive and hard evidence, it's going to be tough to prove it. Even I, who think he did it, will never be sure. But the thing that kind of brought it to the surface of my mind, made me face it, was the bikes."

"The bikes?"

"I went over there and looked in the garage and saw their fancy bikes, helmets and goggles. And I remembered how cyclists whizz by me when I drive down from the country on weekends. Simon could have killed her, taken her body up north in the back of the Volvo station-wagon, along with a bike, and then cycled back to town and gone to the party."

Tom had no trouble believing Simon had killed Georgia. "Being married to Georgia, for a guy like Simon, I bet she drove him crazy."

"What do you mean?"

"Well, she was so good. It had to get on his nerves. What if she found out about Ariela? I can't see Georgia getting nasty like you're doing."

"Thanks," said Jane sarcastically. But she thought Tom was right. Georgia wouldn't be taking small revenges and recovering her self-respect by finding ways to put down her lover. Georgia would understand and be compassionate.

"Maybe I should talk to Simon," Jane said. "Maybe I should face him and tell him what I think."

"Talk to him? Are you thinking he'd confess just because he likes you? That's crazy. And dangerous. I can't let you do that."

"Be careful, Tom. Don't speak to me like that. Things aren't the same between us now. And even when they were, it wasn't ever a question of you letting me do things."

"I'm sorry, I'm sorry," he said, looking down, his face so sad Jane thought he might be about to cry. "I know I've really screwed things up between us. I never meant to hurt you, Jane. I love you. I don't want to lose you."

"It's kind of late for that."

"What do you mean?"

Jane could not bear to see Tom looking so shamefaced and humiliated. Her anger towards him lessened, but her pain was still too great for her to even think of how they might put things back together.

"Simon is crushed with guilt," she said. "Everything he's said and done since Georgia died points to that. But it doesn't look as if he's ever going to admit what he's done or face up to it."

"Well, you can understand that."

"Can I?" Jane leaned back in her chair and closed her eyes. In her mind's eye she saw Simon's sad, worn suffering face and felt compassion. But then she thought about how he'd used her. Why else had he asked her to search into Georgia's death except to avert suspicion from himself? Or had he done it out of some twisted desire that she find out what had happened and understand? Surely, either way, he had been playing with her. But what could she do about it?

"I don't want to be mixed up in solving any more murders," Jane said. "I made up my mind that if I got this one figured out I'd pass it along to

Barrodale. The last one I solved put my business career into a nosedive. If I solve another, people will start to think any company I get mixed up with is going to have an executive knocked off. I told Barrodale what I suspected, although I didn't tell him about the bike. But unless the police find some new evidence, my suspicions aren't going to lead anywhere. If Simon did it, he's going to get away with it—unless I do something."

"What you're thinking is too dangerous, Jane. You might spook him."

"You think he'll try to kill me? I don't see it."

"Jane, if you're right, if he killed Georgia, you can't really know him. You can't predict what he'll do."

They sat in silence. "I think I have to go and talk to him, tell him what I suspect."

"Let me do it. Let me do it for you," Tom said.

"No."

"It makes more sense. I've known him for years. Why not?"

Why not? Jane thought. How like you. You want to protect me and be a hero. You want to love me and be in love with me. But what you don't want is to let me be and to trust me. What you don't want to do is be faithful or promise to be faithful. It's much easier to be a hero. Then she thought that probably it wasn't easier—it wasn't easier to be a hero. Nothing in all this was easy.

"I'm not all that keen on you doing anything for me right now," Jane said. "I'm sorry, but that's how it is."

Tom got up suddenly, gave her an angry look and then left, slamming the front door.

You forgot to say goodbye, Tom, Jane thought sadly. But after everything else, it doesn't matter any more.

CHAPTER 29

After Tom left, Jane walked restlessly around her apartment, unable to sit down, unable to concentrate, trying to decide what to do. Tom had been no help. Her mind jumped from one problem to another without resolving anything. She thought of her relationship with Tom. What was she going to do? Did she still love him? She didn't want to lose him, yet she knew things had changed fundamentally. Tom was not the man she thought he was, so who was it that she loved? She didn't know the answer. Unable to think of a solution, she turned to the problem of her children.

She went into the bedroom she kept for the boys, a room she normally avoided. How I miss them, she thought. She realized that some part of her had dreamed that she and Tom would make a home for the children. Now she faced the fact that that was not going to happen. Time was passing, every day in her children's life was another day gone by that she was not a part of. The emptiness of the room, the outgrown toys reproached her. I will do whatever it takes, she thought suddenly.

Why am I fighting Bernie? It's wrong. What I want is to see my children, to be part of their growing up, to be a mother to them, to give them love and let them know that I care. I'm going to take what I can get. I'll tell the lawyer if the best we can get is Bernie's offer, then we'll take it. I'll go where they are. Being with Bernie and Madeleine. . . . I'll do it, that's all. I'll call the lawyer first thing tomorrow morning.

Having made this decision, Jane felt stronger. She would face up to what she had to do about Simon too: she would think it out, decide what had to be done—and then do it.

It was the bicycle in Simon's garage—that was what had triggered her realization. She had suddenly seen how he could have done it. Murdered Georgia the day of the party, perhaps just before dinner time. Driven her up north in her Volvo station-wagon with his bike in the back. Hidden the car and body in the bush, the valuables in a tree. Cycled back, concealed in helmet and goggles. Of course, the bicycle only put her last doubts to rest. The realization that Georgia had not been at the party, her understanding of the levels of self-deception in herself, in Tom and in Simon, had all merged together. The evidence of those bicycles— the woman's bike dusty, the other not—had only confirmed suspicions that she had been unwilling to face.

The phone rang. It was a telephone solicitor wanting to sell her carpet cleaning. Jane banged the receiver down and began pacing again. She had to do something, but what? If she were right—

and now she was certain—how could Simon's guilt ever be proved? What if there were no way to prove it? Would Simon be able to spend the rest of his life knowing that she knew? Would she be able to stand never knowing for sure why he had done it?

The phone rang again. It was Ivor. "Jane, I'm calling because I've just finished a long meeting with Red and Catherine, and we wanted you to know what we decided."

"Yes?"

"We're with you. We'll sign the agreements, too. No problem."

Jane felt a sudden gust of euphoria, which faded quickly as she remembered her more important problems. "Does that mean I'll have your complete support? No more of this constant undertow, no more passive resistance, no more arguments?"

"Yes, yes, that's what I'm telling you. We've agreed. We'll back you and you can count on us completely. And Jane, I'm sorry about what I did, going into your office. I can see how bad that must have looked. We'll work with you, Jane. After all, we are all on the same side."

"That's great, Ivor. I look forward to seeing the three of you tomorrow to discuss this. And I promise I'll take your ideas into account. We'll work together."

She hung up and the phone rang again. It was Simon. "Jane?" His voice sounded peculiar, high and tense. She could barely recognize it. "Can you get over here right now? Tom is with me and he's said some things I think you ought to hear."

"What? Let me speak to him."

Tom came on the phone. He, too, sounded upset.

"Tom, what's going on over there? What are you doing?"

"Stay out of it, Jane. I'm taking care of it."

"The hell you are!" Jane heard Simon say.

"I'm on my way," Jane said, banging the phone down. She grabbed her purse and keys and raced down the stairs.

It was obvious to Jane as soon as she walked into Simon's living-room that both men were in a rage. "Was this your idea, Jane? Was it?" Simon said, his face as white as paper, his mouth pressed in, so that his lips had almost disappeared.

"No," Jane said, returning his look as calmly as she could.

"Do you think I killed Georgia?"

"Did you, Simon?" Jane said gently. "If you did, I can understand how it might have happened."

"What?" He was standing just inside the door. Now he reached out and drew her in roughly and pushed her into a chair. "Sit down, I want to talk to you. And you, Tom, get the hell out of here. It's obvious she put you up to this. I want to talk to Jane and I don't want you around. I'm going to get to the bottom of this. I'm going to find out how come someone I trusted thinks I murdered my wife."

Tom looked at Jane. "I can't leave Jane here alone with you; that's not on, Arnott."

"Yes you can," Jane said. "You better go, Tom."

"No way."

"I said you better go, and I mean it. Simon is right. I owe it to him to tell him what this is all about to his face." She was now very frightened, but she held her ground.

"You don't owe him shit!"

"Tom, considering how things are between us, I think you better leave when I say I want you to. Do you hear me?"

He gave her a look of despair. "I'll be right outside, Arnott, remember that!" Then he was gone, the door banging loudly behind him.

"Now Jane—" Simon began.

"Don't bother, Simon," Jane said tiredly. "I just can't stand it any more—the lies, the self-deceit. Not mine, not Tom's, not yours. Let's not waste our time with that stuff, okay? Believe me, I know. I see your face and I know."

He sank down on the sofa across from her and put his head in his hands and began to cry. His sobs were loud and rough, the sounds of someone unused to crying; they seemed to be wrenched out of his chest like the coughing of a dying man.

"Anyway," Jane said, watching him, "I probably know what happened."

He looked up at her, his face wet and distorted. "How could you? I don't, and I was there."

"What happened? She found out something about you—was that how it started?"

His voice was very soft, almost inaudible, his expression bewildered. "It was the day of the party. We were going to have an early dinner first. She was standing at the kitchen sink, peeling potatoes, she liked to cook dinner, you know, she—"

"Simon!"

"She was just standing there, with her back to me, and she said, 'You don't have to worry, I know about Ariela,' and she kept peeling those potatoes, peel, peel, peel, and she said 'It's okay, I understand.' And then she started on another potato. I just went into this incredible rage—I was shaking her, my hands around her throat, I was telling her to shut up and then . . . I realized she was dead."

Jane shuddered. Although she thought she had been sure, although she had imagined the scene almost as Simon had described it, hearing him say the words chilled her. Her body grew cold and she realized that she was shivering. "I can understand that," she said, trying to draw him out, keep him talking. "Then what happened?"

"I needed a plan. Georgia was dead. And people would think that I killed her. I had to do something. How would I ever explain? I mean . . . nothing could bring her back, nothing could undo it. And I never meant to hurt her."

"Of course you didn't, Simon," Jane said, forcing herself to meet his eyes with a small smile. "What did you do?"

"I thought of the party. I could make everyone think she was there so that it would seem as if she disappeared right after, a time when I could set up an alibi. I knew I could do that. Fool everybody. After all, that's what we do for a living in the advertising business—create images. It was easy. But that thing with Ariela . . . I'll never forgive myself. That was disgusting, with Georgia, lying where I left her, dead. It's disgusting."

"Why bring me in, Simon? Why ask me to find her when you knew she was dead?"

"I didn't want her to be dead!"

"I don't believe you, Simon. That's no answer."

"Oh God, it should never have happened. I said it was my fault, after it happened, but it wasn't, not really—it was her fault. Do you know what I mean? Somehow, I guess I thought, Jane will find out things that will explain it. It knew if you could find other people who wanted her dead, I'd be safer, and it wouldn't feel so bad. I guess it sounds kind of crazy."

"Just a little," Jane said sadly. Her sympathy for Simon was not totally feigned. It came from a part of her that understood him only too well. "You have to tell Sgt Barrodale about this, Simon."

"I can't do that, Jane. Surely you can see, it wasn't my fault. It was an accident. But the police will never believe it. My life will be over."

"Simon, the only thing that will even begin to make this right is for you to tell the police yourself."

"How can I do that? They won't believe me, I know they won't. They'll think I planned the whole thing. Oh God, how did this ever happen to me?" He looked at her, his face inexpressibly sad. "You believe me, don't you, Jane? You'll tell everybody it wasn't my fault. It just happened. No reason. I knew from the beginning if anyone could understand, you could. You knew Georgia, you knew how hard it was to live up to her."

Now Jane was crying too. Torn between her horror over what Simon had done, and why, and her understanding of it and disgust. She stood up, walked over to Simon and touched him awkwardly; it took all her will-power to do it. "Tell Barrodale and take whatever happens. It's the only thing to do," she said.

Then she went outside to where Tom was waiting.

CHAPTER 30

Simon had confessed, and everyone who knew her role in the confession thought Jane was wonderful. He had gone to see Barrodale, waived his rights to a lawyer and told the whole story. Now that he had a lawyer, he was still insisting on pleading guilty. Barrodale was as close to ecstatic as such a phlegmatic man could be. He said Jane had performed like a seasoned interrogator, pretending to sympathize, to say that anyone would have done the same thing.

Jane had tried to demur, to say it hadn't happened like that, but Barrodale had paid no attention. Still, he had agreed to take all the credit for getting Simon to confess.

Tom had been very graceful about how things had worked out. He had told Jane that now he could see that she had been right to insist that she was the one to confront Simon with his guilt and right, too, in her certainty that no harm could come to her from Simon. But she did not know if he was sincere or if he was only trying to say what would please her. She was still seeing him, still sleeping with him, but there was a distance between them that seemed unbridgeable. Jane was not sure if they could put it back together. She felt a coldness towards Tom that she knew wounded him and that she thought would eventually drive him away.

Malcolm was pleased. Jane had found a manager for the Crystal project and had left it in good shape, on schedule for its fall launch. He had promised her that she would be well rewarded.

There was wonderful news about the children. After intense negotiations between her lawyers and Bernie's, she was going to see them. Bernie and Madeleine would be at their house in St-Paul-de-Vence for the summer and Jane was going to spend her holidays there. She had not taken holidays for three years and Orloff had agreed to her being away for six weeks—though he had given her an assignment or two to carry out in France. But the best part was that she had talked to the boys on the telephone and they had seemed ecstatic about her coming. "Papa said you wouldn't want to come and see us," they had told her, "but we knew you would come." She had done the right thing. She felt very glad about that and she felt joy that she would soon see her sons. The inevitable presence of Bernie and Madeleine—and all that entailed—she was now sure she could handle.

Her happiness about her children made it easier to bear the strong feelings of regret she had over the way things had turned out with Georgia. But of course, she thought as she prepared herself to report to Orloff, she could not have expected murder to have a happy ending.

When she came into Orloff's office, she was surprised to see that he was not sitting behind his desk as usual. He was seated on the leather sofa at the far end of the room. On the coffee-table in front of him was a silver ice bucket, a bottle of vodka encased in a cylinder of ice, and two small chilled glasses. He gestured her to a chair, poured out a vodka and handed her one. "Cheers, Tregar. Drink up."

Jane was not fond of vodka. She took the icy glass and sipped gently.

"No, not like that. Like this." He put the glass to his lips, tipped his head back and drained the glass. He looked at her, one eyebrow raised, a slight smile at the corners of his mouth, daring her. She took a deep breath, then followed his example. Her face flushed hot and she felt the vodka burn in her throat.

He poured them each another, set his glass down on the table and looked at her. "Well? Aren't you going to say I told you so?"

Jane looked down at her hands, waiting for the resentment and hostility Orloff usually aroused in her to surface and give her strength. But this did not happen. Instead she felt a sudden anxiety. Perhaps it was the vodka. What was he up to now? Was this where he told her that despite the commendations of Malcolm Morton and her success at Prospero, she had no claim to a senior partnership? Was this where he made some cruel remark about Georgia?

"It looks like Georgia Arnott was as you thought," Orloff said. His voice had a reflective tone she had never heard before. "Is that right?"

Jane sipped her vodka, thinking about his question, thinking how complicated the answer was, and how she could never even begin to explain it to him. "Are we celebrating, Eddie? Is that what this is? We're celebrating that Georgia is dead and that the husband, who loved her, killed her? And that I got the firm a good client out of it?"

Orloff looked at her, a long, steady thoughtful look. "Actually," he said, "we're not celebrating your cleverness, we're celebrating mine."

"What do you mean?"

"We're celebrating the fact that I'm so clever in bullying and threatening the feisty Ms Tregar that she has again outdone herself and, this time, earned a senior partnership."

"What?" She took a gulp of her vodka. "I don't get it."

"No, I know you don't. That's what I like about it. I toyed with you, Tregar. I poked the right spots and you jumped."

"Did I, Eddie?"

"I've talked to Malcolm Morton. He thinks very highly of you. He's going to retain us to act for all of the companies he directly controls, and to work with him on any new companies he acquires and staffs. That's major business, Tregar. I'm so pleased I'm not even going to ask you how you did it. I'm even going to admit that for a woman you're a pretty tough player."

Jane was so astonished to hear what sounded

almost like compliments from Eddie Orloff that she was incapable of replying.

"Thanks are in order when someone gets a senior partnership, you know."

So Orloff thought that it was he who had driven her to take on the responsibilities at Prospero, he who had driven her to hang in, he who had toughened her so that she was strong enough to win the battles at Prospero. What a joke. And because he now thought she was his handiwork, he was rewarding her with the promotion she had so wanted, the one that she had been sure would offer the security she needed. How ironic. Everyone thought she had triumphed. And only she, now understanding Georgia's death, thought she had lost.

"Thank you, Eddie. Of course I'm very happy."

"You don't look very happy."

Jane smiled, looking into his cold grey eyes, seeing that for the first time he felt some kinship with her. "Of course I'm happy. It looks like I'm finally where I belong."

She raised her glass and drained the vodka. "What more could anyone want?"